MW01173339

IF YOU HOLD ME

CIARA KNIGHT

DEFY THE DARK PUBLISHING

If You Hold Me
Book IV
Sugar Maple Series
Copyright ©2021 by Ciara Knight

Cover art by Yocla Cover Designs
Edited by Bev Katz Rosenbaum
Copy Edit by Jenny Rarden
Proofreading by Rachel

****To receive a FREE starter library (Two free books) AND an alert of Ciara's next book releases, go to Ciara's Exclusive Reader group at ciaraknight.com

❀ Created with Vellum

READER LEVEL

Dear Reader,

I'll tell you a secret.

I was nervous about writing this series. Even after the first book was released and the reviews were great, I still wasn't sure about it. It wasn't until I realized how much all the readers are enjoying it that I relaxed. One of the great things about this series is that the number one reviews these books have received is: "Wow, I love this book even more than the last!" As a matter of fact, I received a surprise from my editors stating how much they enjoyed the story you're about to read. That isn't something I expect when I open the edits to all the red marks and questions about what's on the paper.

This book almost didn't happen. When I sent it to my content editor, I was so nervous because I swore years ago that I'd never write a sports romance. Of course, mine is more small town than sports, but still, I broke my promise to myself. I'm not sure why, but Tanner wouldn't let it be any other way. He was born to be all about football. He's pushy that way.

I hope you enjoy this story about small town sweethearts reuniting after a decade of lies and football have kept them apart.

Happy Reading,

Ciara

CHAPTER ONE

MARY-BETH RICHARDS WIPED off the residue on her Maple Grounds coffee shop counter, wishing she could wipe away the memories as easily. Memories of promised happily ever afters.

"You're doing it again," Andy, her little brother, shouted, as if she were the one with the Air Pods blasting music in her ears.

"Doing what?" she asked, plopping the sponge unceremoniously into the sink and wiping her hands on her apron before she retrieved five mugs for her afternoon meeting. She already knew how it would go with her four friends gossiping about wedding plans and boyfriends and past sins.

Andy pulled one white earphone out of his ear. "You're stress cleaning to get ready for the friend attack. Why do you hang out with the girls if they make you so crazy? I mean, come on, they were childhood friends. I don't get why the town is so crazy about the infamous Fabulous Five. Especially after Judas Jackie stole Carissa's fiancé after high school."

"Old news, buddy. We're all good now that Carissa is

engaged to Drew." Mary-Beth thanked the dear Lord for that miracle. "I don't know what you're talking about, anyway. I'm looking forward to spending time with them. They're like extended family to me." She started on the drinks, closing her eyes and thinking about each girl and what she liked.

Andy harrumphed. "They'll be your only wannabe family when I head to college next year. You'll finally be free of your forced parental responsibilities. Yay to the 'rents for dumping me on you, huh?" He snagged his football from the chair and a muffin from the fridge before he slipped his letterman jacket on and headed for the door, probably to meet up with his secret girlfriend he refused to tell her about. Wow, did he remind her of her own epic high school relationship, the way he strutted around like the Football God of Sugar Maple.

"I wouldn't have it any other way. Andy, you know I begged for them to let you stay with me when Dad got the job transfer."

"Chill. Stop being such a Chad." Andy offered a backhand wave, leaving Mary-Beth feeling like she should lay down some house rules.

"Be back here by nine when I close up."

"See you at ten."

"Andy. I mean it." Did she pull off the "mom" voice?

He slipped on his Aviator sunglasses but tipped them down in that oh-so-familiar jock way and said, "Football, remember?"

"Right. Okay, see you at ten." Feeling like she'd read the Cliff's Notes for Parenting High School Boys instead of the five-volume manual, she sighed and returned to what she did best, making coffee. Each brew was distinctive—sophisticated for Jackie, sweet for Carissa, bitter with a hint of sugar for Stella, fresh and uplifting for Felicia.

The Sugar Maple Courthouse clock tower struck three, warning her that all four of her friends would be arriving for their Fabulous Five Operation Wedding Decorations.

Through the front window, Mary-Beth watched Jackie click across the town square in her skyscraper designer heels, like a model racing for her monthly ration of fat-free, sugar-free, taste-free chocolate-covered celery stalk. But she wasn't a fashion model. She wasn't racing. And she wasn't free. Like Mary-Beth, she secretly held on to the past to avoid the future. Jackie was prickly but a good friend who loaned Mary-Beth designer clothes and constantly told her to stop wearing too much jewelry. Jackie paused at the front steps, waiting for the others to catch-up, wrapping a garland like a boa around her neck and holding a bag at her side. A sophisticated cappuccino with a hint of fresh-shaved hazelnut and a dash of Ceylon Cinnamon waited in her place by the side window, where a crisp fall breeze floated inside.

The opposite in attitude and fashion sense was Sassy Stella, who pulled up in her 1957 Chevy wearing combat boots, faux leather jacket, and heaps of in-your-face attitude. With one glance at the I-don't-care grin on her face, Mary-Beth was sure she'd perfected the bitter coffee with a dollop of almond whipped cream stirred into a white swirl. The girl would never drink something with bling. Stella was the shield in Mary-Beth's life. The one who always had her back and would break down doors and men to keep her safe.

She inhaled the hint of pumpkin from Carissa's cup. Sweet, sensible creation that fit her dependable baker friend's soul. The girl was only a call away.

In the middle, between Stella and Jackie, Mary-Beth placed Felicia, the negotiator of the group. Her London Fog made with lavender and a hint of lemon would provide a brightness with a hint of calm. The perfect pick-me-up after working at her nursery in the drizzling rain all morning.

Fall brought all sorts of weather. Most people thought of it as the end of summer, but Mary-Beth always thought of it as the beginning of hot beverage season. Her favorite season.

The bell over the door jingled their arrival, and as if staged, they each snagged their drinks for a whiff, a sip, and a smile.

"Ah, the Coffee Whisperer strikes again. Perfection." Felicia settled in, laying out leaves in the center of the table.

Jackie dropped the garland next to the pile of vibrant oranges and yellows and placed the bag on the floor by her side. "You are too southern, girl. Always ready to please with a beverage and a smile."

"Thanks. I'm glad you all enjoy my drinks enough to want to meet here. I needed to be available when Andy had a break between school and football." Mary-Beth settled between Carissa and Stella. "Let's get started."

"You know you're the most amazing sister-turned-parent ever." Sweet Carissa's diamond ring flashed under the LED-lighted chandelier overhead. The girl beamed brighter than any piece of jewelry since her proposal to Drew Lancaster.

"I try, but raising a high school boy wasn't part of my life plans. Still, I don't mind. It allowed him to graduate here and not have to move with my father's job transfer. It won't be long before he's off for college."

"How's it being back around the old football field? I mean, all those memories for you and all." Jackie didn't even try to hide her attempt at fishing into Mary-Beth's romantic life, but Mary-Beth wouldn't even nibble.

"Carissa, it won't be long before we're planning your

wedding to Drew and Stella's to Knox." Mary-Beth elbowed Stella, ignoring her glower.

"No making a fuss over my wedding. Knox and I'll go to the Justice of the Peace or maybe have you all come to the garage for a ceremony."

"Please." Jackie rolled her eyes. "Doesn't Knox owe it to his fans to film the wedding? He's the number-one internet sensation in the world now. How you two ever ended up together is beyond my imagination."

Stella shoved an orange leaf into the garland next to another orange one, sending Jackie into a panic.

She flipped her auburn hair behind her shoulder and snagged the epic error away from Stella, who had no doubt done it on purpose just to annoy Jackie. It didn't take much to make her mad these days, though. "Not like that. Didn't you learn patterns in kindergarten?"

"I don't know, did you learn how to share?" Stella shot back.

Negotiator Felicia jumped into the center of the not-so-friendly friendship circle. "I think Ms. Horton is going to love all our efforts. Especially since we're a team again. Sweet Carissa is making the most delicious cake, Jackie did the dress, Stella is helping put together the decorations at the McCadden Farm, and Mary-Beth is organizing everything at the farm."

"And you're doing all the flowers." Mary-Beth added to the list before everyone gave her the sorrowful glance of lost loves and hopeless romantic notions.

"How you dealing with being on the farm?" Stella asked.

The table jolted, telling Mary-Beth someone had kicked Stella into submission.

"Stop. All of you, that was forever ago. I've moved on." Mary-Beth looked across the table. "Now Jackie, though..."

Jackie held up her hand, as if trying to win a fly-swatting competition. "No. I'm not on trial here. We're not having Ms. Horton's wedding on *my* ex-boyfriend's farm." Jackie adjusted the leaves that Carissa had added and made them even more beautiful. That was her gift. Making things pretty.

"Please, he won't even be there." Mary-Beth lifted her own cup to her lips. "He's been gone forever and a month." Even as the words left her lips, she wondered how she'd make it through watching someone else marry on the spot she'd thought would be her wedding venue one day.

"A farm you thought you'd be living at for the rest of your life," Jackie shot back.

Mary-Beth felt her hackles rise. "Maybe you'd be less prickly if you were to try dating."

"Maybe you should take your own advice."

Felicia cleared her throat. "You know, Declan took me to a great place in Creekside a few weeks ago."

Poor girl tried to keep the peace, but she was going to develop an ulcer if she wasn't careful, always negotiating the Fabulous Five drama. "Sounds nice. Maybe I'll ask my date tonight if we can go there next time," Mary-Beth announced to let Jackie know how wrong she was.

"This is date three tonight, right?" Jackie asked.

Mary-Beth eyed the cups. "Yeah, so?"

"We chipped in for a three-date gift." Jackie's expression morphed from combative to pleasant way too fast.

Mary-Beth's hair stood on the back of her neck in warning of a friendship ambush. "That's sweet of you, but I don't need anything."

"Oh, I think you'll need these."

Jackie opened the shoebox to unveil two pink, bedazzled, bejeweled, bewilderingly decorated tennis shoes. "Ah...thanks?"

"She figured you'd need these since you always run after the third date," Stella said in an abrupt, I'm-not-sure-you-got-the-joke tone.

"I understand the purpose."

"I tell you what. Let's make this interesting." Jackie's evil grin made Mary-Beth stiffen. "You run from Seth, a guy you said after date one you thought you liked, then you have to wear these for one entire day in public."

"And if I go on a fourth date, you have to go on one date with someone here in Sugar Maple of our choice."

"Please, you'll never go on a fourth date with anyone."

"At least I go on dates. Unlike some people, I've moved on."

"Ouch, southern girl's been taking some lessons from me," Stella mumbled under her breath but loud enough for all to hear.

Jackie shoved the shoes across the table and snagged her purse. "I don't date because I'm not staying. I have plans for my life. But it's a deal. That's how confident I am you won't make it through a fourth date."

"It's been over a year. When will you admit you're not returning to the big city?" Mary-Beth asked but instantly wished she could pull her words back. They'd been friends without fail. Mary-Beth had even stayed by her side during the epic Judas Jackie man-stealing incident.

Jackie stiffened, her chin shot high, and she gathered her things.

Mary-Beth twirled her earring, trying to think of something witty to change the subject but decided on humble words instead. "I'm sorry. I didn't mean to. I know it's got to be harder to get over a divorce than a high school sweetheart running off for a college scholarship."

Jackie pointed at the garland. "Make sure to finish that before you leave. I need to get to an appointment with a distributor for my new winter line."

"Jackie, come on. I didn't mean to hurt you." Guilt ravished Mary-Beth, so she followed Jackie to the door.

Jackie paused, her gaze fixed out the front windows.

Mary-Beth yearned to make everything better for Jackie, but how do you repair a marriage that took down Jackie's business and her heart all before she knew what was happening?

"I know that," Jackie said. "I'm sorry, too."

"For what?" Mary-Beth eyed Jackie, feeling a hint of warning creeping up from inside.

The roar of a bike echoed through the town square, and Jackie faced Mary-Beth with a questioning gaze. "I guess we're about to see how well you're really over Tanner McCadden."

Mary-Beth's muscles tightened, twisted, and turned her inside out. "What do you mean?"

Jackie pointed to a man unsaddling his Harley. He turned with the unmistakable *football God, crowd pleasing, I'm-going-to-own-your-heart, sexy, haunting, lopsided* grin.

CHAPTER TWO

LEAVES CANOPIED the town square in rich crimson and yellow. Tanner had forgotten how beautiful Sugar Maple could be, with its rich vegetation and small-town charm. He removed his helmet, set it on the seat, and ran his hands through his disheveled, sweaty hair from the last four hours of driving.

The square looked familiar yet foreign, with new storefronts, more businesses, and new residents he didn't recognize. That's what happened when you avoided home for over a decade. Townspeople fluttered around the area, some gossiping about the dangerous stranger invading their territory, others pointing with a hint of recognition in their eyes. If he could've entered town incognito and ghosted away in the night, he would have, but that wasn't going to be an option. Not with his brother deployed, his father gone, and his mom alone to run the entire farm.

He rubbed the pain in his chest. The one that reared up each time he thought of his father's death. They'd been close once, before the man practically threw Tanner out of the tree house before he'd learned to fly. Sure, he'd come to his college football games until Tanner lost his scholarship and his father's dream of Tanner making it to the NFL. After that, Dad had turned his back on his biggest disappointment, his eldest son.

"Well, if it isn't Tanner, as we live, breathe, and I thought we'd probably die before he'd ever bless us with his presence again." None other than Jaqueline Raynor strutted out the door of a coffeehouse with all the drama of a superstar attending an awards ceremony, and he had a feeling that he was about to witness a grand performance.

"Heya, Jackie." He unzipped his jacket and slid it from his shoulders, buying himself a minute to prepare for whatever she was about to sling his way. His brother had filled him in on some stuff before he'd been shipped out, shortly after Tanner had left for college, and it sounded like the Fabulous Five had declared war on him. Well, the four since Mary-Beth had left for college before he could even pack for his own new life. Somehow, some way, he was labeled the bad guy, despite the fact that after they quarreled one time over his choice to attend Notre Dame instead of the University of Tennessee, she'd taken off without a word or phone call, and cut him out of her life forever. He'd been the one to try to patch things up, but she'd never answered any of his calls, text messages, notes. Nothing. She had ghosted him.

"Still sporting the I'm-so-sexy-no-one-can-be-mad-at-me smile?" Jackie struck a pose with one ankle out, flipped coat behind her, and a hand on her hip.

He wanted to remind the woman that her dear friend was the villain in the high school saga of Sugar Maple, not him. "Trust me, I'm not trying to sport anything to anyone. I'm just here to pick something up for my mom, and then I'm headed to the farm. I plan to be as distant and invisible as possible."

"Really? By riding into town on a motorcycle everyone can hear, a James Dean look for everyone to notice, and all staged in the heart of the town. In front of Mary-Beth's coffee shop?"

"What?" His gut clenched as if catching a fifty-yard pass in the end zone of life. "She's gone, left Sugar Maple before I did for her dream life of being a dancer."

Jackie laughed, a sinister, dainty laugh that sounded like a Scarlett O'Hara Joker. "Riiiight. So, you had no idea that she returned to Sugar Maple after college to help her parents when her mother became ill?"

His mind rolled with confusion and fear. "Ill? Is Mrs. Richards okay?"

"Yes, she is now, but apparently Mary-Beth decided to stay and open this place." She pointed to the Maple Grounds sign in swirly, fall-colored font with a large maple leaf at the side. The style screamed Mary-Beth Richards.

He eyed the front windows. Part of him wanted to burst through the doors and demand to know why she took off without a word. Another part of him wanted to get on his bike and race out of town. "I thought she wouldn't be here."

"You would've known if the almighty football hero would've ever taken a minute to check in with his family and friends."

He studied his riding boots. "I'm no hero." That was it, the end of the conversation. No way in God's great Smoky Mountains would he open up to Jackie and the Fabulous Five's impending invasion. He'd go to the farm and hide out until he could escape again when his brother finished up his tour. Only a few months. What could happen in a few months? "Nice to see you again Jackie." He bolted to the feed store and marched to the counter. "I'm here to pick up an order for the McCadden Farm."

"If it isn't Tanner McCadden. Good to see you, man. You really did escape the small-town life. What are you doing back here?" asked a man around his age who looked vaguely familiar with his flat-top, broad shoulders, and square jaw, but Tanner couldn't place him except for recognizing he was an obvious ex-football buddy.

"Good to see you. Sorry, in a bit of a hurry. Thanks." He snagged the feed bag and bolted out of the store, keeping his head down all the way to his bike.

"You gonna put that over your shoulder and balance it there all the way back to the farm?"

He looked up to find a mesmerizing, life-altering, perfectly packaged girl with big earrings, big bracelets, big eyes, and big attitude sitting on his bike. "Hi, Mary-Beth. How you been?"

"I've been here. You?"

"Fine." He adjusted the feed bag on his shoulder, realizing he'd been so busy worrying about getting through town without running into anyone, he hadn't thought about how he'd get the feed bag home on his new motorcycle. The one he bought in Nashville so he could have his own ride without investing too much in a car. He'd lived near campus and rented a car when needed on weekends. He'd been saving for some property outside of town for the last five years.

"Fine?" Mary-Beth placed one hand on the clutch and eyed him with the strangest expression. "I was sorry about your father."

"Thanks."

"I was more sorry you couldn't be bothered to come to his funeral."

Ouch. He dug his nails into the bag and fought his need to yell at the world. "I didn't know."

She tilted her head, and her brown hair with blonde highlights fell over her cheeks as her brows furrowed. "You didn't know?"

"No, I didn't. Not until two weeks after the funeral." He cleared his throat and mind of the anguish he felt at not seeing his father before he'd passed. No way he'd show anyone how much he cared for a man who didn't want him around after his epic football fail.

"Your mom didn't tell you?"

"No."

She rose from the bike and studied him, from his hair to his toes. "But you're here now, why?"

"To save the family farm. That's right, I gave up my life to come save a place where I never belonged and for a man who never wanted me there."

She shook her head. "I don't understand. Your mom didn't tell you about your father, but she told you about the farm?"

"No."

She blinked, appearing as confused as he felt. He balanced the feed bag with one hand and slid a letter from his inside jacket pocket and held it out to her.

A breeze swept through town, sending her skirt twirling around her long legs and her hair across her face. A memory flashed of standing at the edge of a Smoky Mountain cliff with wind barreling through the valley, holding her hand, promising forever to each other.

"It's typed and unsigned. Who wrote this?"

"Don't know. My mom doesn't know, either, but when I told her about it, she broke down and cried for an hour. Now I'm here." He took the note and shoved it back in its spot next to his heart. "I don't know if I want to thank the person or curse him." He retrieved the bag and slid past her, ignoring the pull he'd always felt anytime he was near Mary-Beth. The longing to hold her, to kiss her, to love her split his heart in half.

She placed a hand on his, stalling him. "Wait."

His pulse revved louder than his new bike. "No. I have to go." He needed to flee before he fell apart and begged her to tell him why she'd left, returned, and never told him. Never once spoken to him, never thought to wait for him. Then a spark of excitement ignited inside him. "Did you send the letter?"

Mary-Beth let him go. "I wouldn't have known where to send it." She stepped away from him, her voice dipping to a cool temperature. "I'll get Felicia to drop the feed off in an hour since she needs to be out there anyway."

The last thing he wanted was to see another one of the Fabulous Five. "It's fine. I'll figure it out. I wouldn't want her to make a special trip."

"She won't be, since she has to be out there along with all of us."

His mouth went winter dry. "Why would you all be at the farm?"

"Your mom didn't tell you? We'll be spending a lot of time there over the next few weeks, getting ready for the wedding."

His insides iced over, and he thought he'd fall to his knees. But he wouldn't. He would never let her see how she'd destroyed him, ruined all other women he dated because he could never forget her. Dropping the bag before the weight took his weak knees to the ground, he then slid on his jacket, his helmet, and mounted his bike. "Thank Felicia for me." He pointed to the bag and then revved his engine. His stomach burned with anguish, but he wouldn't let her know how he really felt. "And congratulations on your upcoming nuptials."

CHAPTER THREE

Mary-Beth and Felicia lifted the heavy feed bag and carried it together to the barn at the McCadden Farm.

"You know, Tanner could've carried this for us so we don't pull a muscle or something," Felicia said, winded and bent in half over the bag they'd heaved over the buckets near the horse stalls.

"We don't need his help." Mary-Beth wouldn't ask for assistance from a guy who'd had his father send her away. Mr. McCadden's words still haunted her. *"Sorry, but fame and fortune mean more to him than being with you."* Tanner had been too much of a coward to tell her himself, which made the sting of it even worse. One argument, and he'd split without a word. They'd vowed to attend University of Tennessee together, but then he was offered the big scholarship for Notre Dame and ran off without her. He didn't even consider her or their promises to each other. Poof, he was gone, and she was left behind and forgotten. All for Tanner McCadden to achieve his football star dreams.

Felicia stood, stretching her back. "You're going to have to speak to him on occasion, so why don't you just tell him off and get it over with? I mean, you've been holding it in for over a decade. You're going to explode."

"That doesn't sound like you," Mary-Beth said.

Felicia shrugged. "Maybe Declan is rubbing off on me, or maybe I don't like people messing with my friends. He abandoned you for football without even thinking about the future you both had planned together. It would've been one thing if he'd tried to make it right, to make a plan to see you or talk to you about how it might work out long distance, but he didn't. He only vanished. The coward."

Mary-Beth thought for a minute about Felicia's new boyfriend. They'd misjudged the ex-con profoundly. Apparently Mary-Beth wasn't a good judge of character. The man had been nothing but kind to all in Sugar Maple, despite their prejudice. Maybe that's why he and Felicia worked so well together... Both faced adversity due to their past—Felicia for being born from a mixed-race couple, and Declan for being born to a deadbeat dad who'd let him take the fall for his embezzlement. "Doesn't matter. I'd have to care to hold anything in. And I don't." She swiped the barn dust from her brow with her flannel sleeve and spied through the decaying wood slats of the barn to check for any sign of Tanner before she waltzed outside.

Felicia followed at her heels. "Why don't I get Mrs. McCadden to help with the plants? You can head home to be with Andy."

"He's still at football practice. I have until ten. And I already closed the coffee shop for the day since it's Monday." Mary-Beth slid two potted plants from the back of the truck and carried them to the garden—an old, abandoned, dried-up, wilted garden that needed major tending, but if anyone could transform it by the wedding, it was Felicia. "I'll help, but you'll have to direct me."

"No worries. My amazing boyfriend sketched my ideas into an official plan."

Mary-Beth smiled, and this time it wasn't forced. She was genuinely happy that Felicia had found an amazing boyfriend who worked harder than any man she'd ever met. He'd swooped in, saving her nursery, her grandmother from a fire, and Felicia from a lonely life.

"Wait a second…" Felicia set her own plants down on a wooden bench at the edge of the garden. The bench where Tanner had etched their initials on the back, in the center of a heart. "You can't be here; you're supposed to be on a date."

"Nope. That was canceled."

"Canceled? Since an hour ago?"

Mary-Beth shrugged, knowing that negotiator Felicia would overanalyze the situation.

"Since Tanner rode back into town…into your life?"

"Stop. Tanner has nothing to do with it. The date just didn't happen."

"Really? So, Seth canceled on you? The man who keeps hanging out in town just to take you out on dates?"

"Work. He's here to work." Mary-Beth hotfooted it back to the truck for the next load, but she wasn't fast enough. Felicia blocked her at the tailgate.

"Oh no, you don't. You hold up. No way, no how. *You* canceled that date."

"You're making too much out of it. Seth was…was…too into himself. I don't need another one of those."

"You think every man is too into himself. Even the preacher who dedicated his life to helping children out of abusive situations. Listen, I know how hard it is to face a man who broke your heart, but hon, you need to do this. Think of Tanner returning to this farm as an opportunity, a blessing to help you move on with your life. I know you don't want to. I know it will hurt. But I know you need to do this. And so do you." Felicia plopped her hand onto Mary-Beth's shoulder. "Besides, if you don't talk to him, Davey might send out the minions to tar and southernize him."

Mary-Beth giggled, not from happiness, but more from a dark place that made her pleased at such a notion. "Would that be such a bad idea?"

"Now that you mention it, if you get the syrup, I can get the leaves, and Davey will stand watch as Tanner writes hundreds of apologies to you to stick to himself."

"No thanks. I don't need any grand gestures of love. It worked for Drew to win over Carissa, but honestly, I don't even like sticky syrup."

"What?" Felicia offered faux shock for extra emphasis. "A Sugar Maple resident who doesn't like syrup? Oh hon, you better not say such things. There are ears everywhere."

"I'd laugh, but there's truth to that. I'm glad we're friends and you'll keep my secret."

"Always." Felicia snagged a few more plants and slipped to the side, allowing Mary-Beth to grab her own load. "You know, Tanner will figure out pretty quick that you're not the one getting married."

Her breath quickened from the labor or from the thought of Tanner thinking she had moved on without him. "I'm sure he already knows. Certainly his mother will tell him." Mary-Beth kept her attention on her work, not allowing it to roam down memory lane through the nearby wooded trail that lead out to *their* cliff, or to their secret tree house hideout, or to the roof of the front porch where they'd look up at the stars most

Friday nights after the football games, talking about their dreams.

"Do you remember when we were all kids and we climbed to the top of the large oak over at the lake so you could watch Tanner play football without anyone knowing we were there, because you were grounded and not allowed to leave your room?"

"Don't remember." A flash of the memory tried to break through Mary-Beth's carefully constructed grief-blocking front line of defense.

"You slipped, and your bracelet caught on a branch. We thought you'd lose your entire arm, the way you were dangling and screaming."

"Still don't remember." Mary-Beth set the plants down and went for another load.

"You don't remember how Tanner dropped the ball five yards from the goal, climbed the fence, and saved you, causing them to lose, wrecking their undefeated season?"

"Nope."

"We were what? Ten?"

"Thirteen."

"But you don't remember." Felicia laughed so loud Mary-Beth was sure it was intentional to draw Tanner out of the house. His bike sat near the barn, but he was nowhere to be found. The lights were low in the house and the curtains drawn. "You said you'd marry that boy one day because anyone who would choose you over winning a football game deserved your undying love."

She took a deep breath and decided it was time to make her friend understand why she didn't want anything to do with Tanner McCadden. "That was a boy who chose me over a game. The man didn't."

The words were bitter and raw and nauseating. Her stomach tightened, and she returned to work for no other reason than to move forward, the way she'd been moving forward since she'd left behind the dream of a life that would never be.

For the time it took to finish unloading and for Felicia to roll out the plans Declan had drawn for her, she didn't speak.

As if a flood of questions burst through the dam of caution, Felicia crossed her arms and faced Mary-Beth. "You don't know that he chose football over you. You don't know that he wouldn't choose you now. You don't know if he's the boy from childhood, the guy from high school, or a new man. You don't know anything. And you'll never know anything until you speak to Tanner McCadden."

"No. There's no reason. Why would I ever want to speak to him? There's nothing between us. He chose being a football star over us."

"Because, Mary-Beth Richards, you need to figure out if you're still in love with Tanner McCadden. That's a question anyone should want to know the answer to."

"I know I do." Tanner's deep voice demolished the hint of calm Mary-Beth had managed to hold on to for the last twenty minutes. She turned to find the tall, handsome, wide-eyed heartbreaker waiting for her answer.

CHAPTER FOUR

THE SUNRISE ERUPTED over the mountains like a beautiful bomb. Tanner had forgotten how colorful and alive his hometown was in the Blue Ridge Mountains where the mystic haze settled in during the early hours and the smoky fog at night. The animals, insects, trees, people… All were vibrant and memorable. Once, he'd thought after a few years of pro ball, he'd retire here with Mary-Beth to raise their children. He'd play long enough to make his father proud, secure his financial future, and enjoy the fame but then return to take over the family business, supplying much-needed funds. Now, he wanted to be anywhere but McCadden Farm and the impending wedding. Especially after Mary-Beth let him know the answer to Felicia's question directly. Mary-Beth had no love for him, and Felicia was out of her mind for ever asking her. She'd moved on. Of course she'd moved on! She was getting married to another man…

He shoved the barn door open and faced the first stall that once housed his favorite horse. She'd been gone for years, though. His freshman fall semester at college, he'd received an email stating that his favorite equine companion had succumbed to illness. That was a dark year. The year he'd lost his ability to play ball, he'd lost his future, and he'd lost his relationship with his father.

Brushing off the past and the thought of Mary-Beth getting married, Tanner took the new horse out to the pasture to graze and run while he mucked the stall. Hard work used to make him feel like he was worthy. His father had taught him at an early age the value of manual labor, and he'd taken that with him while working his way through college and ultimately landing a job at the University of Tennessee as an assistant coach. He'd thought that would be a consolation prize for his father, but he had never attended a single game.

Tanner found the wheelbarrow in the same place they'd always kept it and chucked in a five-prong pitchfork he found hanging on the wall. That was new. While he was at it, he grabbed the broad shovel, stable broom, and work gloves. If he was going to do the job, he might as well do it right.

The two other horses in their stalls neighed, as if ordering him to tend to them, too. Based on the amount of manure and wet straw, they all needed attention. How long had the farm been in this condition? His father hadn't been gone long enough for this kind of neglect. The familiar pinch at his sternum warned him of the grief he still hadn't allowed himself to feel over the loss of his father, and now wasn't the time. Not when so many witnesses were watching and gossiping on the farm.

He drove the pitchfork into the bedding and dumped the wet straw and manure into the barrel then scraped any clean hay to the side. After thirty minutes, he realized there wasn't enough clean hay left to make it worth the effort and decided to chuck the rest of it.

Despite the cool breeze outside, the barn was warm. He removed his outer layer, hanging his flannel shirt on the nail sticking out of the pole, and returned to work. An hour passed with two stalls done. His white tank was drenched in sweat, and he was parched.

"It's been a while since you worked on a farm." Mary-Beth's voice shattered his quiet morning with the promise of anger and bitterness he didn't need. "I wouldn't have bothered you, but I need the fertilizer that Felicia left in the storeroom. I'll be out of your way in a minute."

She bolted down the center of the barn to the back corner, with her brown and golden waves bouncing from a ponytail and her boots scraping the floor.

"You lift that nose any higher, and you'll hit the peak of the roof." He couldn't help himself. The resentment surfaced, and he wasn't in the mood to deal with an ex-girlfriend he'd be forced to face daily until his brother came home.

"Me? You're the one who doesn't want to grace any of us with your almighty presence. I mean, come on, I never took you for a coward until now."

Her bottom lip quivered, but she bit it into submission the way she always had when she was so angry, she could cry. She hurried away and opened the storage room door.

She didn't have the right to be angry. That firmly rested in his end zone, so he tossed the pitchfork to the ground and marched after Mary-Beth. "I'm not avoiding. I'm working, trying to get this farm back into shape. The barn roof needs repairs, the stalls are disgusting, the house is falling apart, the pasture is overgrown, vegetable garden dead, not to mention the fact it's almost time to harvest and none of the equipment is running. So, excuse me if I don't have time to help plan your wedding. No one's going to help get this place back into shape but me." His anger boiled to the surface along with the stinging taste of Mary-Beth marrying another man.

"Not my wedding," Mary-Beth mumbled.

His heart reached his throat with a leap of unwanted joy. "What?"

"Ms. Horton—Mayor Horton to you. It's her wedding to Mr. Strickland. I assumed you knew by now." She tugged and yanked at the oversize fertilizer bag that didn't budge.

Energy that he wasn't expecting renewed, as if he'd taken a dip in the lake. The southern gentleman way he was raised wouldn't allow him to ignore her need, despite how he felt about her, so he crowded in between her and a shelf to reach the fertilizer. The storage room was even more confining and hot than the barn. He picked up the bag and slung it over his shoulder. "Where does it need to go?"

"Drop it. I'll get it. You're too busy to be bothered with a wedding." She pointed to the ground, her *too big to be working on the farm* earrings swayed.

"Don't be ridiculous," he said, his tone softer than before, as if the news had doused his anger to embers. "All I'm saying is that this entire place now rests on my shoulders and I have a lot of work to do. No one else is going to help run this place. I'm not being rude. I'm just too busy to help with some event."

She crossed her arms over her chest and tapped her foot. "Why do you think that Ms. Horton demanded to have the wedding at your farm?"

The dull warmth flickered into a skin-warming heat. "How should I know?"

"It doesn't take a genius to figure out that she was probably the one who sent you that letter, and she's probably the one who sacrificed whatever dream wedding she's been waiting to have for like forty years to help utilize town members and small businesses to get this place back to some sort of functioning farm." Mary-Beth poked her finger to his tight abs from holding the heavy bag and narrowed her gaze at him. "So, no, Tanner, I don't need you now or ever, so drop that fertilizer."

So, he did. He tossed it to the ground at her feet, about-faced, and returned to work. What gave her the right to speak to him that way? How would he know why Mayor Horton did anything she did? He'd never had the same relationship with the woman as the girls had. All he knew about her was what he saw at the occasional social gathering and whatever Mary-Beth had told him.

He shoveled and wheeled out two loads of waste while listening to the sliding noise, but he couldn't see the petite, five-foot-four Mary-Beth over the wood stall frame. The only thing visible was her fancy hair clip bobbing up and down. Then the noise stopped, and he decided to make sure she hadn't passed out or fallen or something, but she hadn't. She was holding on to the corner of the bag, using all her body weight to drag it a few inches at a time.

"You're just as stubborn now as you were when we were kids. Move." Not able to watch the woman struggle any longer —and hoping for a little peace in his barn—he lifted her into the air and set her down behind him and then settled the bag over his shoulder.

"I told you I got it."

"You can get it outside." He marched out the door, grumbling under his breath. "Would've been easier to let me do it in the first place, but noooo. Mary-Beth has to always be right."

"I don't always need to be right. I just usually am."

He dropped the bag next to Felicia and Carissa, squatting next to the bench. "Really? Like you were right when you decided we should skip out of math class, sure we'd never get caught, so we could go fishing, and we ended up with poison ivy? Or when you decided that you wanted to be strawberry blonde and you insisted on doing it yourself, and you ended up pumpkin orange? Or maybe when you were right about—"

"Enough. You've made your point. I might be stubborn, but at least I don't run out on people and I don't care more about myself than the people who fed and clothed me, who did without and died early so their precious son could live the football dream."

A coldness flooded him. "You don't know what you're talking about. And this conversation's over. I'm done being judged by you and this town. I'm tired of being blamed for all your poor decisions. Most of all, I'm tired of you."

CHAPTER FIVE

THE DAY WAS long and the night even longer, especially with the girls discussing everything except the dramatic garden episode with Tanner. How was Mary-Beth ever going to get through this wedding with him living on the farm?

She lifted the metal cup to the milk frothier, despite the knot between her shoulder blades. At least she had her coffee shop to keep her busy all day with a solid excuse not to help with anything at the farm until later in the evening.

"Good morning to the best sister in the world." Andy settled onto a bar stool with his bright blue eyes, sandy-blond hair, and an I'm-about-to-manipulate-you grin.

She was not in the mood for games. "No."

"Wow, way to parent. You don't even know what I'm going to ask." Andy swiveled in the stool, plastering on his best three-legged, preemie puppy look he could manage.

"That charming smile of yours works well with most girls, but I'm your sister and I see right through it. Whatever it is, the answer's no."

He held his football to his chest the way Tanner always did

in high school. Did every jock have to keep his identity with him 24-7? Andy slept with his ball on his nightstand as if it would disappear from his life if he separated from it. "You need to study more and spend less time on football."

"I have straight A's. How much more should I study?" Andy chuckled. "But you make a good point. You know how you're always saying I shouldn't rely on football for my future and that I should work on my grades more?"

She set the metal cup down and wiped the milk off the frother, trying to speed ahead to his next turn to prepare herself. "Yeah..."

"Well, I got an A on my test in calculus yesterday. The highest grade in the class. Doesn't that deserve a reward?"

"You're not going to the beach for spring break."

"Geesh, who pissed in your Cheerios this morning?" Andy sat back away from her. "It wasn't about spring break." He hopped off the stool. "I'll talk to you after school."

She sighed and tossed her rag down. "No, go ahead. I'm listening."

"Fine, but I need you to have an open mind. This is vital to my future, and it won't cost Mom and Dad any money, It would help with a college scholarship, and it's only one little, simple conversation you'll have with someone. It's not a big deal at all."

Her faux-parenting alarm she'd been developing rang loud and clear with warning. "Then why are you making it feel like a mega deal?"

He threw the ball up in a spiral and caught it in his arms. "It's not. You can just be...funny about things sometimes. I don't want you to go all girl-monthly-crazy on me or anything."

"First off, never say that again. If you say that to a girl who isn't your sister, I hope she knocks you down in front of the entire team."

He held up his ball at her in mock surrender.

"Spit it out or move on." Mary-Beth realized her espresso shot had burned from sitting there too long, so she threw it out and packed some more grounds to make another one.

"I just need you to ask Tanner McCadden to coach football this year since our coach left without notice and we don't have anyone to step in."

The steam from her espresso machine didn't reach the degrees that scorched her insides. "No. The school will replace your coach."

Andy cradled the ball like an infant against his chest. "They're trying, but as of right now, they are talking about Old Man Praetor coaching. Could you imagine? I'm not even sure his scooter can reach the fifty-yard line. Why would we settle for him when we have a football star coach right here in town? And I know he'll do it for you."

"You don't know anything." She recalled how well things went with Tanner yesterday at the farm, and her determination to hide in the coffee shop to avoid him was a solid plan. "Besides, I have no more pull than anyone else. If the school wants him, they should ask him."

"That's what I told them, but they figured he'd never agree, so they're searching more viable options. But then I told them my sister used to date him, and—"

"And nothing. Tell them to call the farm and ask for him. He'll either do it or he won't. It won't make a difference if I ask him. In fact, based on his behavior toward me the last time I saw him, I'd say I'd harm more than help your chances."

"Come on. I promise to pull straight A's for the rest of the year. I'll even pretend to study more."

"No."

"Why?"

"Because I said so." In that moment, Mary-Beth realized why her mother had used that exact phrase so many times.

He stood there for a moment staring at her. "Ooooooh, you still have a thing for him. Is this one of those sappy movie situations where you never got over the guy?"

"Don't be ridiculous. He means nothing to me. He's been out of my life forever." She mixed her latte and headed for the back office so she could get her stuff to open up for the morning. She had trouble tying the apron with her shaking hands.

"You do. You *so* still like him. Great. Is that why you came back after college? For him?"

"No, for the family. To help Mom when she was sick. Besides, I love Sugar Maple. I belong here."

"Good for you. I want nothing more than to get out, so help me. If you don't have any feelings for him anymore, then prove it. Go ask him for me."

"I don't have to prove anything." She unlocked the front doors, even though she wasn't due to open for another fifteen minutes. "Besides, I'm the last person who should ask him. I might have accused him of being a coward."

"You *might have*? The way I heard it, you did everything but accuse him of being a traitor to Sugar Maple. Oh wait, you did that, too." Andy snagged his backpack from the stool at the front counter. "Go apologize and ask him. For me. Mary-Beth, seriously, this means everything to me. It's my dream to play college ball, and with his coaching, connections, and name, I'd have a real shot." He leaned his head on her shoulder. "Please? For your favorite brother?"

She gulped a huge swallow of hot latte that burned going down. "I don't think—"

"Don't you always tell me that pride is a sin and it's going to cost me more than I want to pay in life? Didn't you make me apologize to Nathan when I called him a wannabe water boy after a game? Are you going to be one of *those* parents? The kind that doesn't lead by example but just manipulates and orders me around? Are you going to be Mom?"

"That's a lower-than-low blow." That was the one thing that drove them both nuts about their parents, and she'd vowed always to be honest and parent with facts, not guilt trips or twisting of circumstances. "If anyone else ever asked me this, I'd tell them to get lost. You know that, right?"

He nodded but didn't say anything.

That's when she saw it: the honest pleading from his eyes, the this-means-everything-to-me head tilt. How could she squash his dreams because her own never came true? "Fine."

He set the ball down on the counter and wrapped his arms around her, squeezing her tight. A foreign act from her teenage sibling. "That's amazing. You're the best sister—I mean parent—ever."

She shook her head. "I said I'd try. I doubt he'll do anything as a favor to me, but you're right. I don't want to be a hypocrite. I want to parent the right way. Now get to school before I change my mind."

He bolted outside, leaving her with the realization she had to face the one person she never wanted to see again to humble herself by apologizing for what she'd said, despite the fact that she'd meant every word. Tanner McCadden was a coward for running off and never returning home, and nothing he told her could change that truth.

Stella entered the shop with her hand out, ready for her free cup.

"Oh no, not today. You've got to pay." Mary-Beth grabbed

a spoon and the tin cup, ready to concoct the perfect apology beverage for Tanner.

"What?" Stella scratched her cheek. "Okay, here."

Before she could reach into her pocket Marry-Beth said, "Nope I don't want your money. I need you to watch the store for about an hour."

"Um, okay. But Knox is on his way over to talk to you about the coffee segment for his show, remember? You agreed to be the next segment, and then Jackie will be after that so she can be the final big show."

"Oh, right. Well, tell him I need to reschedule."

"Why don't you tell him?" Stella shot back.

"Because he likes you. He won't be mad if you tell him. Everyone will be happy." Mary-Beth stared at the empty cup. "This is important. I need to do something for Andy."

"Everything okay?" Stella asked, settling into a seat.

"Yeah, I just need to make the perfect cup of coffee before I go ask someone for a favor for him."

Stella chuckled. "Well, I'm sure the Coffee Whisperer won't have a problem with that. Maybe Knox should start filming now."

Mary-Beth stood frozen, thinking, analyzing, stressing.

"What's wrong?"

She dropped the spoon into the metal mug with a loud clank. "For the first time, I have no idea what to make for someone." With her hands in her hair, she walked circles around the small kitchen area. "Maybe it's because I'm mad at him. Maybe it's because I'm forced to do something I don't want to, for someone I care about. Maybe I can't bring myself to do it."

"Do what?" Stella asked.

"Ask Tanner to coach high school football. It could mean a

full scholarship for Andy. I can't do this." She stopped and faced her challenge. "I have to, though. Maybe—"

"Maybe you still love him even after all these years and that's why you can't make him a cup of your coffee. You don't want to face rejection again."

That was Stella, always ready to tell you the cold, hard, lie-to-yourself realization that was your truth.

CHAPTER SIX

TANNER SAT on the front porch, so exhausted he didn't bother to rock in his favorite front porch chair because it would require too much energy. He blinked at the streaks of first light across the early morning sky. The sounds of nature nearly lulled him back to sleep, but his mom's stirring inside warned him that work would begin soon. When the screen door opened, he growled with protest and tipped his hat to cover his face. "Not yet. I need five more minutes."

A cup of coffee shot in front of him, and his mom knocked the hat back off his head. "Forgot how tough farm life could be, didn't you?"

Frogs croaked, as if echoing his mom's observation. He lifted his arm and groaned from the tightness all the way through his biceps, around to his deltoids, and up his neck. "I work out. I'm fit. I eat right."

"Yet, you're out of farm shape. You know this life is different than all others. Your father was strong and active for many years because of his work." His mom spoke with pride in her voice. There was nothing more important than work ethic to farmers.

Tanner sipped the bitter, hard-core, man-coffee they always drank on the farm. What he wouldn't do for a softer pick-me-up with a hint of promise drink. Maybe he was city boy soft now. He choked half of the vinegarish-tasting blend down while sitting in the rocker next to his mom.

"Your father would be devastated to have you back here." Her words were strangled and full of sorrow.

Surprised at her moment of uncharacteristic emotion, he studied the trees near the driveway that swayed with a burst of wind coming from the mountains, sending leaves raining over the front lawn. He hunched over, resting his elbows to his thighs, the bitterness of regrets stronger than the coffee. "I know he didn't want me here, but I'm all that the farm has right now."

"Gee thanks." Her tone switched faster than hay igniting from one carelessly tossed match.

He softened his tone. "Sorry. I didn't mean it that way. I meant that Pops made it obvious he never wanted me here."

Her brows knitted tighter than a clove-hitch knot. "That's not true. Your father would've loved to have you here."

He let out an exasperated chortle. "Had a funny way of showing that. He made it obvious that my life wasn't here since I was big enough to climb into a tractor. It was all football, all the time." A spasm in his shoulder challenged his next sip of coffee, but he managed to raise the cup to his lips and take one more swallow before he could force his voice not to catch. "I know I let him down."

His mom leaned forward, the chair creaking with the movement. "You didn't let him down."

"Yeah, right. That's why he never came to see me after I

lost my college scholarship? I wish he could've seen me as more than a failed football player."

She shot forward. "Is that what you think?" She didn't say anything else. She only looked down her nose with a hurt, narrowed-eyed expression.

"What was I supposed to think? You never came to visit me, and there was always an excuse for me not to come home. In a decade, I've only seen you a handful of times. Most of those times were for events in Hawk's life. I knew he was Dad's favorite, but I thought that I could make up for not playing in the NFL by getting a college coaching job."

"I know you're a capable, talented, and smart young man, but you're an idiot." She marched to the screen door. "Your father never cared about football. He only cared about you. He cared that you weren't stuck here, that you'd have choices he never had. Your father wanted to give you the world, not take it away from you."

He opened his mouth to argue further, but when she fled inside the house, he didn't have the energy to chase after her, not if he wanted to get enough work done to make a dent in the ever-growing chore list. Not to mention the fact that when his mom walked away, the conversation ended. Nothing he said or did would ever change that. She was as stubborn as Mary-Beth.

The rooster crowed, announcing the workday needed to begin, so he abandoned his cup in the kitchen sink and set off for a crop and orchard evaluation. Walking the grounds, he tried to focus, but his mom's words kept creeping in, fouling his attention. How could she say that? Did his father really send him away out of some false sense of giving him a better life? What better life could exist than being with family and working alongside them once he'd ruined his big chance?

It didn't matter. This place only offered bad memories and lost family.

After deciding there was enough to harvest between the corn and apples, he headed to work on the old combine. Without it, there wouldn't be any harvesting of corn unless he did it by hand one stalk at a time. He snagged the old toolbox from the barn and went to the outer edge of the field, where Gobbles—his brother Hawk had named her when they were kids—sat broken and rusted.

A car rumbled along the front drive, but he didn't care who came for a visit. Most likely his mom had invited Mayor Horton out to discuss wedding plans. The ones designed in parallel with what he and Mary-Beth had discussed years ago. Did she even remember their relationship and promises to each other?

How things had changed since they were young—the *once high school principal turned second mother to a bunch of teenage girls* now ruled the town and, at the moment, his life on the farm. Wedding planning had taken over his mom's life and turned everyone in town crazy with decorating and beautifying the farm, but that wouldn't pay the bills. The crops would.

That stirred his determination to fix Gobbles, so he set to work assessing all the mechanisms, hoping to fix it himself without having to pay a mechanic. Belts, feeder house, and elevator chain needed replacement, some cracks needed to be welded... All that he could do. A few bearings needed some TLC, but the real problem area appeared at the feeder house floor. It would have to be replaced completely. Great... How much would that cost? He crawled under to check the sieves and straw chopper and realized they needed some attention, too.

"You look like you could use a pick-me-up." Mary-Beth's voice startled him, causing him to hit his head, luckily not on any blades.

He rolled out from underneath, rubbing his skull and blinking through the sharp pain. "What are you doing here? Trying to kill me now?"

"No. I brought you coffee. A special blend just for you." She shoved a cup in his face as if it were medicine for his now-aching head.

He stared up at her, realizing she really had brought him coffee. The aroma covered the odor of oil and rust and disappointment, so he took the proffered drink and leaned against the tire, allowing himself another minute to see straight.

"You need some help with this?" Mary-Beth sounded strange, her voice in the I-want-something tone that she'd reserved for getting her way when they were kids.

He took a sip and grimaced at the overly sugared flavor that made it taste more like a butterscotch milkshake than coffee. "Uck. What's in this? A pound of sweetener?"

"No." Her face turned sunrise pink. "You love caramel."

"Not since high school, and not in my coffee." He handed it back to her.

She snatched it from him with a glower and a huff.

He watched her expression turn from agitated to nauseatingly sweet like her coffee. "What do you want?" he asked, with no room for her to question that he was on to her antics.

She closed her eyes, took a deep breath, and then opened them again. "I forget how well we can read each other. We always could. You're right, I need to ask you for a favor."

"I don't have much time for favors right now. As you can see, I'm a little overwhelmed trying to get this place running again." He removed his cap and wiped his brow. "I don't understand how my father let it get this bad."

"You don't know?" She took a step back and looked at the house, then back to him. "Seriously?"

"Know what?"

She took another step backward until she ran into Gobbles. "It's not my place to tell you. I just assumed you knew."

He closed in on her, not leaving her any room to run. "Tell me."

A hawk squawked and soared down to the corn, fetching something and rising into the sky. She watched the creature as if wishing to fly away with it. "Your father wasn't able to work the farm for over a year."

"Why?"

"Because he'd been sick for years with cancer. He fought it with chemo, but that caused heart problems. He was too weak to work."

"Years? How many years?" Tanner choked on the knowledge that his father had suffered without a word to him.

"He was diagnosed about the time you were injured in college, and Hawk did the early enlistment his senior year in high school and left for the military."

"That long?" Heat rushed over him; his breath caught. "My father was sick all that time and no one told me? What happened to the town family motto?"

"You haven't been a member of this family for a long time." Her eyes misted, but she lifted her chin.

His breath caught and didn't want to release. With his hands to his knees, bent in half and gasping for air, he leaned against the dilapidated old machine. The same machine he'd ridden on his father's lap when he was four. Learned to maintain when he was eight. And learned to drive when he was twelve.

Nothing made sense—not his family, not his life here, not the way Mary-Beth's hand rubbing small circles on his back soothed him the way she always had. "How could he not tell me? My mother, my brother... No one told me."

"I don't know why your mom didn't tell you, but I believe Hawk doesn't know either."

He breathed in deep, stinging breaths until he could stand, despite the throbbing in his head that had intensified. "Why wouldn't she tell him?"

"Rumor in town was that they didn't want to tell Hawk because they didn't want him distracted when his life was in danger. Then after a long battle, your father's passing was sudden. One night he went to sleep, and he didn't wake up. I always thought you didn't care enough to come home."

"Didn't care enough? That's what you think of me?" He gripped the warm metal and squeezed, attempting to rid himself of the anger and sorrow that plagued him without allowing his temper to show.

"I don't know who you are. I thought I knew you, but then when you left and never returned, I assumed you moved on with your life and didn't look back." Her hand returned to him, the familiar-yet-foreign touch from the past stirring something inside him. A feeling. A strange peace he didn't expect. A welcome home feeling.

He flinched, wanting to change the subject. "My mom said something strange this morning about how my father sent me away for a better life."

The town courthouse bell chimed in the distance, a cow mooed, but Mary-Beth didn't say anything, so he continued. "I always thought he'd sent me away to fulfill *his* dreams, and I resented him for it, but that was because I thought he wanted me to be an NFL player to make him proud. I always felt like the only reason he paid me any attention was because I played the game he always wanted to play. That he lived vicariously through me."

"Don't lie to yourself... You wanted to run off and be a football hero as much as your father wanted it for you."

"Maybe, but when it didn't happen, he didn't want me home. I felt like he couldn't look at me."

"And now?" Mary-Beth walked around, swatting at the tall corn stalks.

"I have no idea. I mean, he never spent any time with me unless it had to do with football. I tried to help him in the fields, but most days he'd send me to practice." His hands ached, forcing him to release his fingers, which had been balled into fists by his side. "My father was fighting cancer and never told me. I could've been with him, working this place, helping him through it. If I had been here..." His voice cracked, and he couldn't continue, the thought alone too harsh to face.

CHAPTER SEVEN

TANNER APPEARED BROKEN, a state Mary-Beth had never witnessed in all their lives. "You couldn't have saved your father." She approached him with a soft step, soft touch, soft heart. The anger and resentment she'd been holding melted away. "I knew you felt pressure in high school to get a good college scholarship, but I had no idea you felt that way about your father."

He shrugged. "I didn't. Not until he disappeared on me when I was injured. Like I wasn't good enough to be his son anymore. Had I known he was fighting cancer, I would've insisted on coming home and helping here."

"I'm guessing that's why your father didn't tell you." Mary-Beth still resented the way Tanner had left, but they were kids then and had been friends since they were toddlers. Seeing him in that kind of pain softened her resolve, her bitterness. "You should talk to your mother about how you feel. I'm sure she can tell you more than I can. I was gone for four and a half years for college, and since I returned, I've been busy with the coffeehouse and raising my little brother." She paused, remembering why she'd come to speak to him in the first place.

"What is it?" He scratched his chin the way he'd always done when he was figuring something out. But nowadays, he wore sexy scruff instead of boyish virgin skin.

Mary-Beth shooed him off. "Nothing. It isn't important right now."

He picked up some tools spread around in the grass and tossed them into his father's large red toolbox that had belonged to his grandfather and probably his father before him. There was a lot of history on this farm. That was one of the things she'd always liked about this place. "The favor you were going to ask. What was it?"

She toed the blades of pale green, knowing this wasn't a question she wanted to ask, especially with all he was facing, but it was for her little brother. The one person in her life she'd do anything for, since he'd always been her light when the world was dark.

"You might as well tell me before we start yelling at each other again." He winked, his playful, I'm-going-to-turn-this-situation-around kind of wink. He'd always been good at lightening a mood, which was probably why everyone had loved him in high school. It was a defense mechanism she recognized as a way to avoid pain and uncomfortable feelings. But it wasn't her job to care for him anymore.

"Right. We wouldn't want that again. The town is already talking about our reunion." She pushed her shoulders back and decided to go for it. "You know my little brother is in high school now, right?"

"Right." He wiped his strong, farm-blistered hands on an

oil-stained rag. How he'd changed in the brief time he'd arrived home. The wounds on his hands would pop, hurt, and callous over the coming months, or he'd be gone in a week and they'd return to city soft.

"Well, I think he wants to live up to your legend. He wants to get a big college scholarship for football."

"You want me to talk him out of that?" He smiled, the half-crooked, I-own-your-heart kind of smile. And he always had, until he was gone.

She averted her gaze, refusing to fall for such tactics. "No. If that's what he wants, I won't stand in his way, but there's a problem."

"What's that?" He stiffened, his forearms flexing.

"The high school coach left, and they have no one decent to train them—well, except Mr. Praetor. They should make it to state this year, the first time in almost a decade, and Andy hopes to get noticed by college scouts."

"Old man Praetor? Can he still walk?"

"He uses a scooter most of the time." She shrugged. "Will you do it?"

He slammed the toolbox shut. "Do what? You haven't asked me anything yet."

"Will you coach the high school football team?"

He stood, stretching his arms over his head. "No."

A rippling of anxiety traveled the length of her arms and legs. "No?"

"No." He snagged the toolbox and headed toward the house. "As much as I'd like to help Andy, can't you see I don't have time to eat or sleep, let alone play ball?" At the edge of the field close to the barn, he stopped and eyed the land. "There was a time when all I wanted was to work this land.

Now all I want to do is get away from here. The desire is as dead as this place. After five generations, it's now beyond repair, yet I've been charged with the impossible task of restoring it."

"I can help," she blurted before she could stop herself. What was she doing? The last place she wanted to be was the farm.

With Tanner.

Working side-by-side.

Alone.

"Unless you can fix that combine, the roof of the barn, harvest the land, there isn't much you can do."

She didn't like to be dismissed, and she didn't like letting her brother down. No matter how much she didn't want to be around Tanner and all the feelings that she'd thought were long gone but were bubbling to the surface, she would swallow her pride for Andy. She'd been detoured from her plans to be a dancer on Broadway. She wouldn't let him be dismissed from his ambitions. With phone in hand, she marched to find cell reception at the little spot near the front porch. Once three bars popped up, she dialed.

"Who're you calling?" Tanner approached her with an inquisitive eyebrow lifted.

"I'm more capable than you think. Stop acting like you're all alone. You're in Sugar Maple. Here, you're never alone."

"Hey. What's up?" Stella asked.

Mary-Beth spoke before Tanner could stop her. "You know how you're running a tab at the café? Well, I'm cashing in. Come to the McCadden Farm after I close up shop, and bring your tools. You're going to fix an engine for me."

"What kind of engine?"

She shrugged, as if Stella could see her.

Tanner shook his head. "I don't need any help. I just need to work without interruption."

"The kind that runs a combine to harvest corn."

"Cool. I think I can manage that." She hung up without another word. That was her way, on to the next task without a goodbye. Pleasantries had always made her uncomfortable.

"Okay, now, I freed up enough of your time to go check out the football team after school. I'll meet you at the high school at 3:30 sharp. Don't be late." She hoofed it to her car without looking back.

"I didn't agree to this," he shouted after her.

"I'll have men here Saturday to fix the barn roof, and I'll be here after football practice and after the morning coffee rush to help with harvest and care for the animals."

"Why would any men in town help with the roof? It won't happen. I need to stay here."

She about-faced. "Your excuses are over. The wedding will be here, so they had already spoken about working on the structure of the barn. Again, we're a town family. Despite you abandoning us, we're still here, and we don't turn our backs on anyone. We would've been here sooner, but your father wouldn't accept the help. You call *me* stubborn?"

Without giving him a chance to answer, she hopped into her car and tore out of there. The entire way back, she felt the whiplash of emotions. She'd gone out there to ask for a favor she'd hoped he'd refuse, only to order him to do it anyway. What was she doing?

When she reached the coffee shop, she discovered Carissa and Felicia loitering outside, pretending to walk the town square. "What's going on?"

"We heard," Carissa stood on the curb and looked down at Mary-Beth with sympathetic eyes.

Felicia snagged her in a friend embrace and ushered her into the coffeehouse, as if heat lightning would strike them both on this cloudless fall day. "Tell us what happened. What's going on?"

"I don't know." Mary-Beth collapsed into a chair and eyed her muddy shoes. "One minute I'm convincing myself that I have no choice but to go ask Tanner to coach high school football so that Andy can get a college scholarship but planning on convincing him it's a stupid idea, but then I find myself begging him to do what I don't want him to do. And then I convince him by offering to work side-by-side in the fields with the man who still churns up old feelings, turns me around like a fair ride, and spits me back out to clean up the mess. What am I doing?"

Carissa eased into the chair at her side. "You're working through a lot of feelings you ignored for many years. It's not going to be easy, but I'm glad."

Mary-Beth found herself twisting her bangles so hard she caused her arms to turn red. "What? Why would my torment make you happy?"

Felicia settled in at her other side. "Because, hon, you've never moved on, and we want you to feel what we feel in our lives. That magical person who makes the world brighter, happier, and more fun. You'll never have that as long as you cling to those old feelings you had for Tanner. Now you can work past them."

For the first time in her life, the smell of coffee churned her stomach. "I can't even make a cup of coffee he likes."

"What?" Carissa asked with a hint of confusion.

"Nothing. Never mind. It's not important."

Felicia slid a hand onto her arm. "The Coffee Whisperer finally met her match. No surprise. You have no idea who he is today."

"Did you offer to work with him to get to know him better?" Carissa asked in the softest, barely audible voice.

The room fell silent—not even a car passed outside or a person waved through the window. "Of course not. Tanner McCadden is nothing more than a boy I grew up with who I need to help my little brother. He owes me that much at least, after running off and breaking his promise to me." She shot up and headed for the espresso machine.

"Then there's no reason for you to worry. You're simply helping out an old friend at his farm. Nothing too foreign about that in Sugar Maple. Right?" Felicia offered.

"Right." Mary-Beth snagged a ton of supplies and lined them all up in front of her.

Her friends closed in around the counter. Carissa leaned in, studying all the potential ingredients. "What're you doing?"

"I'm figuring out the perfect cup of coffee for Tanner. It can't be hard. The man's easy to figure out. Small-town football hero runs off for a better life and only returns when he discovers his family farm is failing. Kind of a no-brainer, right? I mean, I'm the Coffee Whisperer being featured on Knox Brevard's show."

"Right," Felicia agreed.

They all stood there staring at the syrups and the milk and the spices.

"So, what's stopping you?" Carissa asked

Mary-Beth dropped her head to the counter and beat her fist near her ear. "I've got nothing. For the first time in my life, I can't even make a cup of coffee, let alone a perfectly crafted beverage for a person." She looked up at her friends, hoping for them to soothe her worries. "What does this mean?"

"You know what it means..." Felicia offered her most sympathetic, sweet, scandalous smile.

"Oh, dear Lord, no. I can't still be in love with Tanner McCadden!"

CHAPTER EIGHT

THE LUNCH BELL on the front porch rang, letting Tanner know that his mom had cooked something up. Part of him didn't want to go inside and face the look he'd received earlier. But the other part of him wanted to know what she'd meant when she had insinuated that his father did want him around and that Tanner had it all wrong.

He snagged his shirt from the post and slid his arms into it, abandoning the back-aching work of fence repair for some sustenance. The aroma of his childhood favorite, steak and cheese sandwiches, wafted from inside. He opened the screen door with a loud squeak. Great... Something else that needed tending to.

"Don't forget to take off your boots. No mud in my house," his mom called from the kitchen.

With one hand to the wood-shingled wall, he kicked off a boot and then the other, trying not to fall face first over the threshold due to his legs spasming. Every inch of his body either had a scrape, bruise, or sore muscle. His mom set his plate at his old kitchen table seat and sat across from him. The head of the table, his father's seat, stood empty, along with his brother's. They'd once shared boisterous meals, but now the kitchen remained muted, old, and worn.

The smell made his stomach noticeably growl in the quiet, so he picked up the hearty sandwich, only to get smacked.

"Where are your manners? Give thanks before you gobble that down."

He felt like he was ten again with the scolding, but he obliged since this was still her house. He clasped his hands together and tried to give thanks but couldn't imagine what to thank their dear Lord for. Their town pastor always said things happened all according to God's plan, but what was his plan with all this? Father dead, mother suffering, land drying up, crops neglected, repairs, and now coaching football? No way. He unclasped his hands and dug into his meal.

With one bite, he melted into his chair and closed his eyes. "No one in the city makes these the way you do."

"Don't talk with food in your mouth, son." She set her napkin in her lap and took a nibble of her own half sandwich. "So, tell me what Mary-Beth came by to talk to you about. She looked nervous and stressed when she arrived."

"Nothing worth mentioning. She just had some crazy idea that I should coach high school football while I'm here."

"Why's that crazy?"

He dropped his sandwich, coughing and gasping until he managed to swallow his bite and some milk. After recovering, he looked at his mom as if she'd been hit by Gobbles and suffered a head injury. "Seriously?"

She placed her sandwich down in a manner befitting the Queen of Bulgaria instead of a farm woman. "Give me three good reasons why you shouldn't."

He matched her posture and ticked off on his fingers. "I don't have time with the work here."

"I'll help, and the town is coming out Saturday to work on some repairs so that it looks nice for Mayor Horton and Mr. Strickland's wedding. And you need a life beyond the farm if you're going to stay."

"I'm not." He took another gulp of milk. "I'm only here until Hawk can return home. He's the one meant to inherit the farm. No way Pops would've left it to me."

"We'll get back to that. That's only one reason. What are the other two?"

He held up the next finger. "I'm a college coach. Why would I coach high school?" He laughed nervously.

"So, you think giving back to the people of this town who lifted you up and gave you opportunities with football don't deserve you? That you're too above these people now?"

"No." He rubbed his forehead, feeling the grit of outside on his skin. "I mean, I'm sure they have someone else to coach a high school team to state. Why me?"

"Why not? You're the best this town has to offer." She took another bite and then wiped her hands. "And the third reason?"

"Do I need another one?"

"You haven't given any valid ones yet. You've given excuses, not reasons. First one, we've already established the town will help. The second, we understand, is that your pride won't let you do it, and the third? I'm guessing has to do with Mary-Beth."

"I don't know what you're talking about." He took a massive bite and chewed the steak like an angry bull.

"You don't? Then give me a valid reason why my son—who I raised to be a loving, caring child with a responsibility to the community —won't go help out a bunch of kids with a dream. A dream he shared once."

The guilt weighed on him. "What if I don't even like football anymore?"

"You've decided you don't like the game? The same game that you obsessed over when you could crawl to the box and pull out the ball to throw and catch before you could stand? The same game that you ate, slept, and devoted every waking hour to as a kid? You know that for sure?"

"No. Not for sure. Coaching college ball as an assistant is too disconnected from the actual game, and if I'm being honest, I think I resent the game. You said that Dad cared about me despite football, but what was I supposed to think? He didn't speak to me from the moment I lost my scholarship."

"It's complicated." She pushed back from the table.

A lump lodged in his throat. "Why didn't you tell me about Pops's condition? All those years. I could've been here to help, to be with him."

Her eyes went wide and her mouth fell open for a second before she closed it and rose from the table. "That's why we didn't want to tell you. Your father and I never had a choice but to remain on this farm. We don't regret the years we spent here, but it was his duty to stay. He wanted you and your brother to have a choice."

"A choice means there were options." He swallowed, but the lump wouldn't move. His eyes misted as he remembered that empty feeling of loneliness and disappointment that had raged and ruled over him for years. "Mom, how do you think I felt when he drove me away after my injury? I was broken and alone and felt like no one cared about me because I wasn't the star we all thought I'd be. It was humbling and horrible."

"We can't change the past. Just know everything your father ever did was out of love." She shot from the kitchen before he could press her further.

It didn't matter, though. She was right about one thing... He couldn't change the past, but what did he want for his future? Football had brought him nothing but disappointment and a wedge between him and his family.

He finished his sandwich and returned to the front porch to put his boots on.

His mom had work gloves on and headed for the herb garden, but she paused. "Just because your dream didn't turn out the way you had hoped, at least you had a shot. From what I understand, Andy has a crap coach and no parents. Try to remember how you felt at seventeen, with the hope of playing college ball even though it was a huge obstacle considering your humble upbringing and the little exposure our town had in the world of football. It took more than just your talent to achieve your dreams of being offered multiple college scholarships. It took your coach, us, your town family, even the town elders, who chipped in for the team to afford the trip to state. All of that isn't being offered to Andy. Are you going to punish him because of how you feel about Mary-Beth?"

He stood there with one boot on, watching his mom walk away in her rolled-up jeans, flannel top, and judgmental gaze. For a second, he allowed himself to think back to those years. Everyone in town had cheered him on, driven him home from practice when his parents couldn't make it, spent extra hours on the field to make sure he was ready for the big game. Mary-Beth always by his side, his biggest fan. His mom was right. He did owe the people of Sugar Maple. If he couldn't pay them back, he could pay it forward to the next kid, even if it was the last thing he wanted to do. This wasn't about him; it was about Andy and his dream to play ball. This time, maybe, the dream would last more than one pass and a tackle.

He finished repairing the fence, changed his shirt, and drove to the high school, but when he reached the parking lot, everything flooded into him at once. The cheers echoed in his head. The smells of game food and sweat. The feeling of catching a pass in the end zone. The congratulatory kisses from Mary-Beth. Kisses that promised him a happy future but only gave him a broken past.

CHAPTER NINE

"I OWE YOU BIG-TIME. I promise to do well in school and help out around the café any chance I get." Andy pounded his football to his chest as if doing some sort of ritual greeting dance for a coach.

"Just work hard on your academics. If not, I pull Tanner from coaching. Got it?"

Andy only nodded, but she didn't think he heard a word she said, with his mesmerized, locked-on gaze at the Sugar Maple football legend approaching.

"If this doesn't work out, you know I'll pay for your college."

"No. You finally paid off your own loans and those to open your shop. I won't put you back in debt." Andy waved her to silence, and now wasn't the time nor the place to argue with him, knowing he would never listen. Not with Tanner strutting to the field with that familiar jock swagger, as if he owned the universe. She knew that swagger made most women swoon at the sight. Not her. She liked the softer side, when they were alone and he made her feel like she was the only woman in the world and he didn't want to be anywhere else but by her side.

Tanner didn't stop until he was too close for comfort. "Hey."

His warm breath breezed across the tip of her nose and over her lips, so she took a step back and shot that perfectly created, hour-long science experiment cup of coffee into his chest.

"I guess I look how I feel. This might actually keep me standing long enough to see what these kids have."

Andy shot between them, offering his hand. "Hi, Coach. Thanks so much for doing this. The guys are all pumped and ready." After their too-long, white-knuckled handshake, Andy took off to the other boys on the field.

"In case you didn't notice, you've made his life. I've never seen him so excited."

Tanner pressed his lips together and shook his head. "Can't believe how much he's grown up. He was what, six last time I saw him?"

"Seven. I missed him every day." She eyed her little brother, the boy who thought she'd given up so much to watch out for him while he finished high school, but truth be told, she couldn't bear the thought of being away from him again.

"You look like a mother about to have an empty nest." He took a swig of the coffee.

She held her breath, but when the cup came down, she saw his lip curl at the edge. "What's wrong? What don't you like about it?"

"It's good. Really." He gave her a condescending pat on the shoulder.

"Good?" She huffed. "Good? I'm the most well-known

barista in the county—no, the state. Maybe the country. I've been nicknamed the Coffee Whisperer. I'm about to be featured on a well-known internet show about my coffee creations."

"I said it was...well, I don't want to say it again since you look like you're about to dump it over my head." He eyed the field. "I better get out there."

"Oh no, you don't. You're not going to escape that easily. Tell me what's wrong with the drink."

He ran his free hand through his thick, dark hair and looked at the cup and then at her. "Nothing. It's just not something I would usually drink."

She wanted to tell him to try it again, but one glance and she saw his clucking tongue trying to free it of the liquid residue. "Be specific, please. What don't you like?"

"I don't know... There's like a grass or hay flavor to this. I can get that while working in the fields or barn."

"Are you saying my beans are under roasted or damaged?" Mary-Beth gritted her teeth. No way she'd allow her beans to go bad. "That's a special, high-quality coffee you're drinking."

"I guess I'm just not a good coffee connoisseur." He handed her back the cup and trotted onto the field, leaving her holding her rejected brew. She sniffed, and it smelled rich and vibrant, but then she sipped it.

Dang if he wasn't right. She stomped off to go investigate how this could've happened. She'd been saving that bag of coffee for months, waiting for the perfect opportunity to use the rated 95 expensive beans.

At her car, she snagged one last look and noticed Tanner's gaze fixed on her the way he used to look at her—with want and desire. Her body trembled.

She shook it off and hopped into the car, ignoring how she

responded to him. Anger crept in at the memory of him never even writing her back or calling her. She put the car in reverse and forced her attention on the road all the way back to Maple Grounds, where she flipped the Open sign over for the evening and went to investigate the coffee bag.

The only way the drink would taste like that is if the mild roast had gone bad, gotten wet, or been old. A few months on the shelf wouldn't cause that flavor. She opened the bag, and it smelled fine. Turned it in all directions to make sure there weren't any holes or water damage. Held it up to look under and discovered the reason. The expiration date was from last year. She'd been so excited to try the coffee, she never thought to check to see if it was out of date.

She sank down to the small stool behind the counter and eyed the expensive splurge that had been too good of a price to pass up. Now she knew why.

The bell rang at the front of the store, and in shuffled the elders for their afternoon tea. She tossed the bag in the trash and went to work brewing, pouring, cutting lemons, and plating some scones from Carissa's bakery she had dropped by earlier.

Davey and Felicia's grandmother, Ms. Hughes, snuggled like two lovebirds in the corner, while Ms. Gina glowered at them and Ms. Melba prattled on about the day. The town elders were all-knowing, plugged in to the Sugar Maple Gossip Hotline. Heck, they'd practically founded it sixty years ago.

Mary-Beth didn't need to suffer the Elder Inquisition, so she painted on her best smile and greeted everyone. "Good afternoon. I have a Darjeeling for Ms. Melba, Earl Grey for Ms. Gina, English Breakfast for Davey, and a mint for Ms. Hughes. Here's the creamer—oh, and Ms. Gina, I included a hint of lavender in it the way you like it." She placed the special tiny white pitcher next to the Earl Grey and retreated.

"Not so fast," Davey hollered after her. "Spill it."

She halted, took a breath, and then turned on her heels to face the inquisitive bunch. "Spill what?"

"What's got you all mixed up and turned around?" Davey said, pointing to the cup in front of him. Shoot, she'd mixed them all up. No way Davey would drink tea with a lemon on the side of his cup. "Oh no, sorry. I'm just tired. You know, raising a teenage boy who is obsessed with football can be exhausting." She flung her hair back for extra drama and then switched the cups around to their correct positions.

"We heard Tanner is coaching Andy. How you feel about that?" Davey asked.

"Fine. It's a great idea. I asked him to do it, you know. Andy deserves the opportunity to get a scholarship. He's really good." Was her tone convincing?

"As good as the legend?" Ms. Melba asked.

"He's better than Tanner." Mary-Beth stuck her nose in the air and marched to the counter.

"Funny, she thought I was talking about Tanner. I meant Charles Frankinslip from 1946."

Mary-Beth refused to be baited into a conversation about Tanner. "That would be a little before my time, you know."

"She's calling us old," Ms. Gina said with a little spittle at the corner of her mouth.

Mary-Beth grabbed a rag and scrubbed all the kitchen surfaces with vigor.

"I bet she's still hung up on that boy and he's gonna break her heart again," Davey said. "Then I'll have to fight him." He put up his tiny, sun-spotted fists and duked it out with the air.

Ms. Gina put a loving hand over his knuckles and lowered

them to the table. "No need. It was the other way around; she broke his heart," Ms. Gina whispered but at a yelling level so she could hear herself.

"Is that what the town thinks? That I chased him away?" She tossed the rag into the sink and bolted to the back room, fuming. What did it matter what the town thought? It was better they didn't know the truth. At this moment, she wished she couldn't see the big picture. Because if she did, she'd have to admit that her friends were right that the man who she'd sworn off years ago still held her past, present, and future hostage in his athletic grip.

No more.

She slid her phone from her pants pocket and texted Seth. "Sorry to cancel our last date. If you're free tomorrow night, I can go out after I'm done helping at the farm. I'll meet you at the coffeehouse at seven."

Three dots danced instantly.

See you then.

And with that one text, she vowed to pry her heart loose. Nothing Tanner could say or do would change the past, and it was time for her to look toward the future.

CHAPTER TEN

THE KIDS WERE PUMPED and worked harder than any of the college students he'd trained over the last several years. Andy was as good, if not better than Tanner had been at his age. He watched the kid run like he had wings on his cleats. The boy was talented and deserved his chance at a college scholarship. But was Andy one tackle away from his career ending before it ever began? Tanner wanted to make sure the boy knew the challenges that faced him, to prepare him the way no one had ever prepared Tanner himself.

When practice ended, he felt a love for the game he'd lost a few years back. The rush he used to experience on the field had returned for the first time since his injury all those years ago. Tanner chalked it up to first day energy and the kids trying to impress their small-town football hero. That would fade if he stuck around. The kids would drag, and he'd find himself making excuses not to attend practice all the time. After all, he had responsibilities at the farm. How could he afford the time to coach high school football? And at some point, he'd return to his assistant coach position. Was it only platitudes, or did the university mean it when they told him they'd welcome him back when he was ready?

Andy tossed the ball at Tanner and removed his helmet. "So, coach? Do you think I have what it takes to snag a college scholarship?"

If the boy understood how loaded that question was, he wouldn't ask Tanner to answer it.

Andy's mood melted in front of him. "You don't?" He deflated as if someone let the air out of his shoulder pads, and Tanner knew he couldn't take the chance at his dreams away from the boy.

"I absolutely think you have what it takes. As a matter of fact, I'll even make a few calls on your behalf."

Andy jumped like he was warming up for a game.

Tanner tossed the ball back to him. "Hold up a minute. I know this is exciting, but I want you to know all the facts before you decide your future. If you want me to make those calls, then we need to have a man-to-man talk."

"Anything. What's up?"

Tanner eyed his watch. "Can't this minute. I need to get back to the farm."

"Tomorrow. Before school. We can meet at the coffee shop." Andy bolted to the locker room before Tanner could argue the point. The boy was floating on dreams and ambition without a thought to the fact his cloud could burst at any moment with no warning, flooding his future full of disappointment.

The principal of Sugar Maple High School and a few men with him, one toting a camera, headed his way. The last thing Tanner wanted was to be in the local paper, so he darted to his bike and tore out of there. The thought of returning to fan admiration made him feel hollow. He'd felt empty for so long. When was the last time he'd felt full?

He shook off the notion of Mary-Beth and focused on the road ahead, winding through the mountain pass and up to the farm, where he found the Sugar Maple gang parked across his front drive. Everyone he'd tried to avoid was standing on his front porch, in his barn, or at his field. Avoidance was no longer an option. He could send them away like his father, the man who'd bullied people to get what he wanted in life, but since when did he want to be like the man who'd kept secrets and told lies? The man he'd once been so close to who had made him feel abandoned and unloved. Had he had a clue what that did to a man?

The crowd gathered, as if waiting for him to catch the winning pass, but all he could do was roll his bike to a stop and remove his helmet. That's when he found himself searching the audience for Mary-Beth, but she was nowhere to be found.

"Welcome home!" Mr. Strickland, the infamous fiancé of Mayor Horton, held out his hand. The man was a legend with the women, but for some reason Mayor Horton had never given up on him and she finally had won him over.

"Good to see you again, sir." Tanner unzipped his jacket and greeted the remaining members of his hometown community. Once the fuss had ended, he made his way into the barn and checked on the roof repairs. To his surprise, the work was going well, so he went to the garden, where he found Felicia and some man working.

"Hi, Tanner. I want to introduce you to my boyfriend, Declan."

The man was large enough to be a linebacker but had a gentleness about him when he looked at Felicia. "Nice to meet you." Declan held up his gloved hands to show why he didn't offer to shake.

Tanner was happy for Felicia. The girl had had it rough growing up. Thank goodness she'd had the Fabulous Five to protect her when the kids were cruel, teasing her because she'd been born from a white mother and a black father. He'd never understood why they'd teased her, since she was so beautiful, but kids were cruel, usually out of jealousy.

"She's in the field working with Stella on the tractor." Felicia winked.

"I wasn't…" He realized his gaze had been everywhere but on the two he was speaking with.

"Weren't you?" She smiled. "Even if you weren't, you should head out there to check on the combine. Last I heard, Stella was cursing and threw a wrench, asking how anyone could treat a machine so poorly."

"Sounds like Stella. And she isn't wrong." He'd thought the same thing when he'd spotted the poor machine for the first time upon his return.

He pushed up his sleeves and headed for the fields. The sun was almost to the edge of the mountaintop in the distance, and the corn stalks waved with the breeze as if to welcome him home. He'd forgotten how beautiful it was in Sugar Maple and how fresh the air smelled compared to anywhere else he'd ever lived. Life had different meaning in the country. It wasn't all fast paced and who's better than who. Instead, it was more friendship and kindness and love.

Clanking of metal sounded before he caught sight of Stella and Mary-Beth. Her hair looked like a fresh wheat field glistening in the sun. He'd dated lots of beautiful women, but they were all enhanced with eyeliner and mascara and special clothes. Mary-Beth was different. Some in the city would call her plain, but he saw the natural beauty that didn't need to be dressed up and paraded around to garner attention. Well, except for her jewelry. She always had loved bling.

"You!" Stella growled. "You best not be coming out here to see if this thing is running yet. I can't believe you left this poor beast out to rust and corrode like this."

Tanner shook his head. "Not me. I wasn't here."

"That's the problem. You abandoned it and—"

"What she means is that this is going to take some time, so don't expected Gobbles to be ready tonight. But I know Stella can work her magic and fix the poor old girl." Mary-Beth shot in front of Stella and shooed him back the way he'd come. "Before I forget, Mayor Horton needs to speak to you. She's in the house."

"You best run. The way you treated this poor girl is unforgivable," Stella shouted after them.

Tanner turned to plead his case, but Mary-Beth snagged his arm to lead him away. Her soft fingers wrapped a quarter of the way around his bicep, and his skin awoke in a distracting rush of warmth. The aroma of espresso and flowers wafted from Mary-Beth, and the chiming of her bracelets sang as they walked toward the house.

"You better stay clear of Stella. I can only use the free coffee card for so long until she loses her temper. You know how she gets when she sees a machine mistreated. I'm not sure, but I think she believes they are living, breathing creatures."

"I remember. Do you think she can fix the old girl?"

"I have no doubt. If I'm the Coffee Whisperer, she's the Machine Whisperer. Of course, I guess I can't claim that title anymore since I can't get your beverage right."

He squeezed his arm, trapping her hand between his ribs

and his bicep to stop her by his side. "You know, a lot went on all those years ago. Things I have a feeling we both probably either regret or we're upset about." He let out a lungful of hot air. "I guess what I'm trying to say is that if we're going to be around each other, maybe we should talk or something."

"You, Mr. Jock, want to talk about feelings?" She laughed.

He pulled away and marched to the back corner of the house. "This was a mistake."

"Wait." Mary-Beth caught up to him and snagged the back of his shirt, pulling him to a stop. "You used to be able to take a joke. Apparently I'll have to be more sensitive in the future."

Tanner didn't like her words, but he didn't try to run either. He wasn't a kid anymore, and even if he wanted to get away from Mary-Beth, he knew it wouldn't work. After all, he'd planned on hiding out at the farm and avoiding all the townspeople until he could escape, and that failed like an interception in the end zone. "Listen, we obviously will have to work together, so that means we'll need to be civil, okay?"

"Civil?" Mary-Beth's bright eyes softened into a sadness he recognized from when they were younger and she'd get a bad grade on a test, or someone picked on one of her friends, or one of the girls flirted with him.

"What?" He faced her and really looked at her for the first time since he'd arrived. And as he'd feared, the sight of her melted his insides and made him want to make the world better for her. He brushed a strand of grass from her chin with his thumb. Her lips parted, and she sucked in a quick breath. Did his touch affect her still the way it had when they were teenagers? That magic was only for high schoolers who lived on hormones and Red Bull. It didn't exist in adulthood. He knew. He'd been chasing after it for years.

"It's just that I thought perhaps we could at least be friends for the sake of the town."

"Were we ever friends?" he asked.

She quirked her head to the side. "I thought we were."

"I mean, we were a couple since before we were old enough to date. I've never thought of you only as a friend since..." He cupped her cheek, and flashes of them kissing by the lake drew him closer. The memories of their love and promises erupted inside him with such intensity, he had to escape. "Never mind."

She let him go, but not without a harsh word to follow him. "As I thought. Always running from something."

He thought about turning around and having it out with her about what happened all those years ago, but the entire town would stand as witness. No, that was a private conversation. A conversation he could have with her in the morning at the coffee shop once Andy left for school but before she opened her doors. A conversation long overdue. At the edge of the house, he cleared his throat but didn't turn to face her. "Tell your brother I'll be at the coffee shop at six in the morning to discuss his future. We'll talk then."

Before he about-faced and took Mary-Beth into his arms to see if his memories could be a reality, if the desire boiling inside him was real or fantasy, he retreated into the house and couldn't help but think Mary-Beth had spoken some sort of truth about him. He could've come home despite his father's protests at some point, but he hadn't. Because he didn't want to face his father's disappointment at his failure in college ball. Perhaps if he had manned up and returned, life would be different for them all. His father might still be alive if he hadn't worked so hard on the farm alone.

For the rest of the day and far into the night, Tanner

allowed himself to think about his past for the first time in years, but he only knew one thing—that returning to Sugar Maple was even more difficult than he'd thought it would be, but it was time for him to start mending the fences of his past or suffer even more regrets in his future.

CHAPTER ELEVEN

A NERVOUS ENERGY and the drying heater that smelled of burned chemicals wouldn't allow Mary-Beth to sleep. It always smelled the first time it ran each year, and since the temperature had dropped last night, it had cut on, if only for a few hours. Once the sun came up, it would be pleasantly cool but not bitterly cold.

The old-fashioned clock Mrs. McCadden had given her for Christmas a long time ago—it had belonged to her mother—clicked away, as if reminding Mary-Beth of every minute she'd spent away from the McCadden Farm over the years.

The clock chimed three, so she tossed off the covers and went to her hope chest. Another item that had been given to her from Mrs. McCadden. This one had appeared after the death of Mr. McCadden, left on the porch at the back entrance of her apartment over the coffee shop with only a note that read:

This should have been yours. And now it is.

The old wooden chest with hand-carved flowers on the lid looked like it had belonged to Mrs. McCadden's grandmother's grandmother. Mary-Beth had always admired it in the front parlor, where she'd sit and have hot cocoa on a fall evening, waiting for Mr. McCadden and Tanner to arrive home from football practice. She'd always been closer to his parents than her own. Probably because both her parents worked so much and Mrs. McCadden was always there. Until she wasn't anymore.

Mary-Beth lifted the lid that creaked from age, and the calming scent of cedar rushed at her with one deep breath. She spotted the artifacts of her high school life with Tanner. The picture book she'd made for him their sophomore year with their childhood visits to the lake, fireworks, picnics, school dances, post middle school and high school football game celebrations, and the town fair. They were children and happy. The way every childhood should be.

Rain drizzled against her bedroom window. She watched the drips streak down the glass. It would be a busy day in the coffee shop since everyone would seek a warm place to huddle out of the weather. This was always the beginning of her busiest season. She needed rest, but if she'd ever be able to sleep again, she needed to work through her ten years of avoidance.

She opened a shoebox to find tossed items and memorabilia inside. Report cards, pictures of her dancing at the local recreation center, acceptance letters to them both for college, her corsage from prom, and handwritten notes they used to leave each other in the metal box inside the secret panel in their old tree house they'd built in the woods between his farm and her childhood home.

The old envelopes were worn but legible, and they chronologized their relationship from third grade to senior year. The handwriting changed, the verbiage matured, but they all read of missing each other when they were apart a few hours, longing for when they'd marry and live together, making their own rules. Naïve childhood promises that they had believed once.

She giggled at the sight of their handwriting in fourth grade. Tanner had teased her that she'd need to be a doctor since only he could decipher her writing. She'd thought about it for a while, but being a doctor wasn't her calling. Business and people were her thing after dance. Besides, she belonged in Sugar Maple. Once she'd realized she couldn't outrun the pain of losing Tanner, there was no reason she'd needed to stay away. Until now.

The letters slipped through her fingers, landing in a trash heap of broken thoughts, and she slammed the hope chest closed. There was no use in returning to bed for her to toss and turn all night, so she dressed and headed downstairs to start prepping for the morning rush. She needed to be done early anyway if she'd be sitting down to speak with Tanner. About what, she had no idea.

Her stomach swished and swooshed, and the only thing that calmed it was activity, so she scrubbed the refrigerator and the espresso machine, wiped down the counters, cleaned the large glass windows, and swept the floor.

She stopped when she spotted herself in the mirror and decided she needed to make herself look like she hadn't been up all night. No reason to let Tanner know how much he still affected her, so she retrieved her makeup bag and dotted some concealer under her eyes, stroked on some mascara, and painted on some lipstick.

Tap. Tap. Tap.

She dropped her powder into the bag and swung around to find a damp Tanner at the front door of Maple Grounds. A quick glance at her watch revealed five in the morning. She shoved the makeup bag behind the computer and hurried to the door. "What on earth are you doing out in the rain and at this hour?"

"I didn't sleep, and I have a full day, so I need a pick-me-up. Figured you had the best coffee in town, right, Coffee Whisperer?"

"You mock me. Why should I let you inside?" She winked but opened the door.

"Because I'm helping you save your brother from a horrible mistake."

She closed and locked the door behind him and grabbed a towel from the kitchen for him to mop his hair and face before he dripped all over her floor. He shrugged off his rain jacket at the door, hung it on the coat rack, and wiped his shoes on the mat like she knew his mama always taught him. "What are you going on about?"

"That's why I wanted to speak with you before I met with him." Tanner rolled up his long sleeves, as if about to dig into some hard labor.

"Oh." She tossed the rag at him, knowing she didn't hide her disappointment well.

"That and about what happened all those years ago and where we stand now. You were right about one thing. I may not have known it, but I was running from this town."

She paused at the second bistro table and eyed the memory-come-home. "You were?"

"Yes." He swiped his face. "But we'll get to that later. How 'bout that cup of coffee and our discussion about Andy first."

"You got it." She eyed the wrought iron leaf pattern in the chair back. "But what do you want?"

He shrugged. "Just coffee, I guess."

She hid behind her espresso machine before he could see her disappointment. That was the problem. He knew her too well, even after all these years.

He slipped into her personal workspace and handed her the coffee filters.

"Thanks."

"Why couldn't you sleep last night?" she asked before grinding the coffee beans with a loud squeal that drowned out his answer. "What?"

"I said because I was thinking about our conversation today," he said at a shout that echoed through the shop.

"About my brother ruining his life?" She busied herself, attempting to keep her mind and hands occupied at all times. Did he know how sexy he looked in the muted light, fresh out of the rain? Why did that man affect her just by entering a room or speaking in that deep, gritty tone?

"Yes, and about us."

She knocked over the metal mug for frothing milk, and it clanged louder than a high-pitched gong on the Chinese New Year. "Oh. Okay, so talk." She chased after it, kicking it twice before retrieving it, washing it, and placing it back on the counter. This time over by the espresso machine where it belonged.

"I know you want me to encourage your brother and help him earn a college football scholarship, but I can't do that in good conscience. Not when I know that course could ruin his life." He paced the kitchen area, running his hand through his dark, wavy hair. He'd always looked sexy with wet, disheveled hair like he'd just walked out of the lake and lay down by her side on a beach towel with water sliding down his chiseled muscles.

"Do you hear me?"

"Yes. I hear you, but I don't understand. You went after the football scholarship. You gave up everything when a full ride came along, without a word to anyone. Why do you want to deprive my brother of something like that? Are you jealous because you don't get to be the hero anymore?"

"Because he could give everything up, only to lose his so-called dream and everything else along with it." He breathed hard, looking like a wild bull stuck in a pen.

She finished pouring the grounds into the basket and turned on the urn to brew before dragging her eyes to his lips that spoke with such passion. "What are you trying to say? That you regret going after your dream?"

"No. Not if it was really my dream. But was it? I mean really. And even if it was, look at how it turned out. Don't you want better for your brother? Don't you want him to have a good life, full of love and family? Trust me, fame and fortune are fleeting and lonely."

She saw it, the regrets and unhappiness behind his chiseled façade. "But then, you wanted the dream when you left high school. I know you did. We talked about it often, and we had a plan. We were young and foolish, but I know one thing... Tanner McCadden would've given up everything to be a football star. Even the woman he vowed to love forever."

CHAPTER TWELVE

HER WORDS of abandonment sucker-punched his gut. He bent over, holding the counter for a moment. "Mary-Beth. No. That's not true." His memory of her never speaking to him again stuck in his brain like a poisoned splinter. "I waited for you. For months."

"What are you talking about? You decided at the last minute to run off to a different school. You told me you were going after the big scholarship, so we broke up and I left."

"Yes...I mean no. Yes, we broke up, but then I came after you and you were gone. That night, I'd left a note... I..." He threw his hands up. What was the point of all this? It wouldn't change anything. "I texted you, but you never responded, so I went to your house, and they said you'd left to go visit campus, but you'd return that Monday, and your parents promised to give you my messages. I waited for weeks to hear from you, but nothing. You never came, you never called, you never responded to my note, my texts, my messages left with your parents. What was I supposed to think?"

"I never got any of them."

They stood there staring at one another for several moments.

"Tanner, you broke up with me. I went to your parents' house to tell you goodbye because I didn't want to leave things between us after that horrible fight. They told me that you were already gone. Your father told me that he was sorry, but sometimes the promise of fame and fortune will change a man, and did I really want to go chase after you, only to be tossed aside later?"

"He said that to you?" Hatred, resentment, and anger rose up, and he wanted to hit something. He turned and punched the wall, sending plaster and dust floating into the air.

"Tanner!"

He rested his head against the wall, his eyes closed. "I'm sorry. I didn't mean to lose it." He breathed through the anger. "I didn't mean to."

"Forget the wall. Your knuckles are bleeding. Come here."

He didn't move. Shame filled him. A temper that he thought he'd left behind in childhood just bubbled back into his life. If there was one thing he never wanted to do, it was to lose his cool in front of Mary-Beth. His father would be ashamed of him.

She rubbed circles on his back, the way she had the night he'd been so mad, he'd punched a kid and sent him to the hospital when they were in middle school. That night, he'd sworn never to hit anyone or anything again. And he hadn't. Until now.

"It's okay. It sounds like we were both manipulated, and that hurts us both."

"That's no excuse." Tanner pushed from the wall and faced her—the bright-eyed beauty who hadn't run away without him, hadn't broken his heart. And despite believing all this time that he was the one who had been mistreated, Mary-Beth had believed that of him. He rested his head to hers. "I didn't and would never have run off without you. Not like that. Not without speaking to you first." He fought the venomous realization of family betrayal. "Our parents. They did this." His muscles tightened, and he wanted to yell or scream or punch something again.

"Shhh." She touched his face, caressing his cheek. "It's in the past. I suspect your father did it out of love to give you the freedom you never had. Mine, I have no idea why they did it. But I intend to find out."

When she pressed her palm to his heart, the stinging in his chest soothed. She'd always had that effect on him. No matter what happened, when she touched him, the world became a perfect place. Their world together had always been perfect.

He wanted to pull her close and promise her the world again, but before he could say a word, she slipped away. If only he could hold her one more time, all would be well.

"Come on. We need to clean up your hand before you bleed all over my floor." Her voice had returned to sounding distant and protective.

"Mary-Beth. I want—"

"Don't. Not right now. There are so many things we probably both want to say, but we need time to process all of this. It's been a decade of thinking you didn't want me, that fame meant more to you than me."

"Never."

Mary-Beth wet the cloth and dabbed it at Tanner's knuckles. The sting made him retract, but she kept hold of his hand. If only she'd kept hold of him ten years ago. "We're seriously not going to talk about it?"

Footsteps stirred overhead, telling Mary-Beth that Andy would be down soon. "Not right now."

"Later, then?" His blood turned the white rag crimson, but the wound wasn't bad. The wall was worse off than his injury.

"Yes."

"This evening, after everyone leaves the farm."

"Sure." She dunked the rag under cold water, her gaze far beyond the sink.

"I'm sorry again about the wall. I'll be here in the morning to fix it. I promise." He allowed her the space she asked for and slumped at the table near the window. His mind flipped through every conversation he'd had with his family, with her, with himself, but he stalled on the night before he'd left. The fight they'd had over his decision to change to the other university, when they had a plan set, housing set, their futures set. He'd gone home, sure he'd done the right thing, believing his father's words that if he and Mary-Beth were meant to be together, they'd both graduate debt free and have an amazing life together. That only lasted until the first rays of light the next day. The day that he went to the store and bought the only ring he could afford and went after her, only to discover she was already gone.

He'd been devastated but had still believed in them enough to place the letter with the ring in their hidden compartment of the tree house for her to find when she returned home. He'd waited for her call, but it had never come.

The back door flew open, so Tanner took a gulp of his coffee and settled in for a chat with a young man he wanted to save from his dreams, but one glance at the boy holding the football, and he knew it was hopeless. He saw himself ten years ago, and no one would've stood in his way.

"Hey, there." Andy bounced with each step, as if he'd already had three cups of coffee before he'd come down.

"Hi." Tanner took another sip, crafting his words carefully. "You know, it won't be easy. You'll have to work like you've never worked before."

"Hard work's not a problem for me. I'm a Richards." Andy tossed the ball up in a spiral and caught it. "I promise, I'll do anything to earn that football scholarship. I can't believe Tanner McCadden's my coach."

"Whoa, I didn't agree to be your coach yet. I simply attended a practice. And before I agree to anything, including making some calls, you need to listen to me."

"I'm listening." The boy's gaze was expectant and excited.

"You know, college won't be just about football. It's about academics. You'll be torn between parties after games and studying for your exams. Without grades, there isn't college."

"Yes, but without football, there's no college for me either. I mean, Mary-Beth will find a way to send me, but she just finished paying off her own student loans. I don't want her going back into debt for me. She found a way to put herself through school. I can too."

"She paid for her own college? I thought your parents said if she didn't...well, it doesn't matter."

"No, they reneged on the whole if-you-dump-your-boyfriend-we'll-pay-for-your-college thing. She was told to come home and help out or pay her own way. She chose to pay her way."

"Of course she did." He wasn't surprised that she'd managed on her own. She'd always been the strongest, bravest woman he'd ever known. "Listen, you understand that you could be injured the first play of your first game. I'm living proof of how a career could end abruptly."

"I know, and if that happens, I'll finish college on loans like you did. Listen, I know you didn't get the dream that you wanted. But that doesn't mean I can't. If you make a call, you'd be doing me a huge solid, man."

Tanner traced the rim of his coffee. "There's no talking you out of college ball?"

"Nope."

He sighed, a decade-long, loss-of-dreams sigh. "Then I'll make the calls. I'll be with you through the entire process to guide you. Do you have any questions for me?"

"Yeah, just one."

"What's that?"

He eyed Mary-Beth, who was working in the kitchen and attempting to appear uninterested in their current conversation. "Are you still in love with my sister?"

CHAPTER THIRTEEN

As Mary-Beth had suspected, the light rain drove people into the coffee shop all morning, and despite the rain stopping by lunchtime, the crowds didn't let up until her afternoon break from two to five. Luckily, she had help coming in to handle the evening shift and closing. It took a lot for her to trust someone to run her coffee shop, but Carissa was going to drop in to check on Mary-Beth's assistant manager, Serena.

When Mary-Beth locked the door at two in the afternoon, she decided to call her mother for a chat before heading to the farm. Mary-Beth wanted all the facts before she could face a wounded-looking Tanner again.

At the realization he might have suffered with their breakup as much as she had, everything she'd believed for a decade had flipped upside down. In that moment of realization, she'd had a plethora of emotions colliding at once: relief, grief, joy, sadness, hope, fear, and so many others. She pulled her cell phone from her jeans pocket and called her mother. Not to Mary-Beth's surprise, it went to voicemail. Her mother was always too busy to chat with her children.

When the phone beeped for her to leave a message, she forced as calm a tone as possible and simply said, "Call me back ASAP. We need to talk."

She grabbed her keys and drove to the farm. Halfway there, just after the bridge, her phone rang. It hadn't taken long to get a response to her message. "Good afternoon, Mother."

"Hello, Mary-Beth. What's going on? Is it Andy?"

Mary-Beth almost felt bad for making her mother worry, but she deserved to be punished for what she'd done to Mary-Beth and Tanner. "No, it's not about Andy."

"Well, what's the emergency? I'm not on an official break and need to get back inside. You wouldn't want me to lose my job."

Mary-Beth forced herself to take a breath before she spoke. "Mother, we need to talk about what you and dad told me when I left for college."

"What are you going on about? Listen, I'll call you after work."

"Did you lie to me and send me away so that you'd break Tanner and me up?" she blurted.

A gasp sounded through the car speaker. "You don't understand. You've never been a parent."

Mary-Beth turned into the McCadden driveway. "That's your answer? So you did lie to me? It's true?"

"Listen, that boy was going to take off on you. Mr. McCadden even warned us that Tanner would be a huge star and then you'd be nothing to him anymore. You couldn't see that he was using you for emotional support, only to toss you to the side when he didn't need you anymore. I was protecting you."

"Is that what you think of your daughter? That I'm not good enough?"

"Don't be ridiculous. That's not what I'm saying. I just wanted to protect my baby girl from heartache."

"That wasn't your choice to make." Mary-Beth pulled to a stop out front and shoved it into park. "My life could've been different," she mumbled, but apparently her mother heard her.

"He didn't come riding back into town in a white limo to win you back, not even after he lost his big, important future."

"That's not fair. He thought I'd chosen to stay at college instead of wanting to be with him."

"And you received your degree and opened your own business. You're doing better than I or your father could ever do. I never wanted you to end up working double shifts or having to choose between paying the electric or your phone bill."

"Money isn't everything, Mother."

"You can only say that because you haven't been without heat or having to decide between feeding your children or paying the mortgage. Listen, when Andy's done with school, we think he should go to college near us. Your dad's new job is paying double what he made in Sugar Maple."

"No, he's going to get a football scholarship and go to a great university. He's got strong grades and potential. You're not going to promise him that you'll pay for his school and then change your mind the way you did with me."

"Not that again. Tell me you're not encouraging him to chase after unrealistic dreams. He's smart. He can go to two years at the local community college, and then Dad and I will be saving to send him to his final two. I know we couldn't pay for your school—things happened, and your dad and I couldn't afford it—but we hope to do two years for Andy."

Mary-Beth shook her head. "Seriously? You took Tanner

away from me, and now you're going to take football away from Andy? Great, Mother. It's funny how you choose when to play parent."

"Listen, you're angry with me right now. Let's talk later. I need to go."

Click.

Mary-Beth rested her head against the steering wheel and closed her eyes. The insanity of her mother nearly drove her mad.

Tap. Tap. Tap.

She looked up to find Mrs. McCadden at her window. "Come on, child. I'll make you some hot cocoa."

Her words were like Sugar Maple syrup poured over a stack of steaming hot cakes—warm, filling, comforting. She slipped from her car and inside the house before anyone working spotted her and gave her the third degree about why Tanner was in her coffee shop at five in the morning. Because there was no doubt they all knew by 5:01.

Inside, Mary-Beth inhaled the smell of old wood and coffee.

"Sit. Relax before you fall down, child." Mrs. McCadden disappeared into the kitchen, leaving Mary-Beth by the window in the parlor, looking at the front field. If she closed an eye, she could make all the cars and commotion disappear, and she could imagine the sound of children laughing and chasing one another. She touched her belly. She'd always thought she'd be a mother by now, living in a home and caring for her family. Sometimes God had other plans, or at least meddling mothers and fathers did.

Pans clinked in the kitchen, and she knew it wouldn't be long, so Mary-Beth thought about what she'd say. It had been different with her own mother, knowing she'd only be blessed with minutes to speak to her, but Mrs. McCadden was different. She took her time and had always made Mary-Beth feel special, important to her. She'd been a member of their family from the time she could ride her bike to their home. And Mrs. McCadden had lost so much recently. Mary-Beth had to be kinder to her but still find out the truth.

How could she have been a part of breaking them up? If Tanner was right, all the parents had been a part of the great lie. A lie that stole their happily ever after from them. Tears pricked at the corner of her eyes. By the time Mrs. McCadden returned to the parlor with two mugs, Mary-Beth could hardly hold in her tears. She knew if she spoke, she'd be harsh, so she bit her lip to keep from verbally attacking a woman she once admired and thought of as a second mother.

"Oh, darling. I'm so sorry. You know, don't you?" Mrs. McCadden collapsed onto the ottoman by her side and handed her a cup. "You have no idea how much I wish things could've been different. If I had known how much you both truly loved each other, I might have fought harder." She held Mary-Beth by the forearm and squeezed. "Please, give me a chance to explain."

Mary-Beth struggled between wanting to know why and not wanting to hear excuses, but in the end, she knew only the truth would matter.

CHAPTER FOURTEEN

THE FIELD REMAINED wet from the early morning showers, but Andy plowed through the linemen, caught the football midair, and trudged through the mucky practice field. The boy wasn't just good. He was gifted.

By the end of practice, Tanner knew it wasn't fair to hold Andy back. Not because of his own issues with the game and how things turned out. This was Andy's life, not his own. He decided then and there he'd call a few college scouts and invite them to their next football game.

"Huddle up!" Tanner yelled.

Most of the team stumbled in on weak legs, sludging through the puddles with slumped shoulders and dragging their helmets. Andy strutted up with his fingers strung through his face mask and muddy water dripping down his face. The conditions didn't even phase him. Tanner remembered that football high, something he still craved but had to face he'd never feel again.

He debriefed the team and dismissed them, knowing he would need more from them next week before their big game against their rivalry team in Creekside. The Sugar Maple High School football team ambled to the locker room, all except an expectant Andy.

"Hey, kid. What's up?" Tanner waited for Andy's obvious questions about scouts.

"You never answered my question." Andy lifted his chin. "I want this chance more than anything, but not at the expense of my sister—the only person in my life who ever took care of me. You going to stay and break her heart again?"

Tanner blinked. His mind raced with possible answers. Raw nerves threatened his temper, so he took a moment, swallowed, and formulated an appropriate answer. "It's admirable that you want to look after your sister, but I'm afraid that is a question I can't answer at this moment."

"Why not?"

"Because it's complicated." Tanner grabbed the equipment bag and slung it over his shoulder.

"It's not complicated that you broke my family when you left. I might have been young, but I still remember my sister crying all night and then leaving the next day, only to return four years later. The day you left broke her heart, and I don't think she's ever been the same. I won't let you do that to her again." Andy squared off with him, and despite the fear in his eyes, he stood his ground, ready to defend his sister's honor. Tanner realized it wasn't fear of picking a fight with Tanner, more his fear of losing his opportunity to play ball for college.

"She cried all night?" Saying those words sliced his heart into meaningless tiny pieces. He'd vowed never to hurt her, only to cause her the worst pain of all. He knew because he'd felt it himself. "Listen, I didn't mean to break your sister's heart. But you should know she broke mine, too. As I said, it's complicated, and I don't know most of the answers right now, but your sister and I are sorting through some of it now."

"What are you talking about?"

"All I know is that our parents lied to us to break us up, but I don't know why. But I intend to find out." Tanner passed the equipment bag to Andy. "Lock this up for me. I need to get to the farm."

Andy opened his mouth in protest, but Tanner shut him down with the one phrase he knew would distract him. "By the way, I'll be calling scouts tomorrow. You've got real talent."

With those words, Andy apparently forgot about defending his sister's honor and took off full speed to the locker room, leaving Tanner to drive home on his motorcycle and think about how to ask his mom to finally tell him everything. Why they'd kept his father's illness from him. Why they didn't even call Tanner when he was going to die. Why they tore Mary-Beth from his life. So many questions needed to be answered.

He drove through town and out the other side, over the bridge, and pulled into his driveway, spotting Mary-Beth's car already parked out front. Good. If his mom wouldn't tell him, maybe she'd explain things to Mary-Beth. They'd always been so close.

With only a wave to the people working on the farm, he darted inside, where he found Mary-Beth sitting in the parlor with an empty cup by her side. "Where's Mom?"

She pointed out the window. "Ms. Horton showed up an hour ago to discuss wedding stuff, and your mother hasn't returned."

He slid off his jacket and tossed it over the chair. "Did you ask her anything about what happened?"

"She said she'd tell me everything, but then Ms. Horton showed up, and I've been waiting ever since. I did speak to my mother, though."

He hesitated, noticing the way she twirled her bracelets like she did every time she was worried or upset. "And what did she say?"

"The typical excuses and quick hang-up before she really had to face anything. Basically, that we weren't good for each other and she wanted me to go on with my life."

He sighed and collapsed into the other chair. "This is messed up. I don't understand how they could've done this to us."

"I don't know, but I get the impression your mother wasn't happy about it either."

"Why do you say that?"

"Because she said she should've fought harder for us." Mary-Beth twisted her feather earrings. "As if she was for our relationship, not for destroying it. But why wouldn't she just tell us the truth, then?"

Tanner glanced out the window and saw his mom approaching. "I don't know, but I think we're about to find out."

At the creak of the screen door, Tanner faced the entryway and waited for his mom to appear.

"Good, you're here, too." She stepped into the room, wringing her hands in front of her. "Can I get you a hot chocolate, son?"

"No, all I want is an explanation. Why did everyone gang up against us, lie to us, and convince us the other one had run off for a better life?"

She gestured for him to sit, and he obliged, despite his nervous energy.

His mom clasped her hands together tightly and took in a deep breath before she began. "You know your father worked here his entire life, never had an option to leave the farm due to family obligations. He wanted to be a dentist when we were young." She gave a half-smile, as if remembering another, happier time. "His grades were strong, but when it came time to go to college, he gave it up to stay here with me, on this farm, working until the day he died." She choked, demolishing Tanner's wall of anger, so he reached out and took her hand.

"He didn't want that for you, Tanner. I told you earlier that he didn't want you to stay at the farm out of obligation, but it's more than that. He didn't want you to always have to work so hard, only to struggle financially all your life. Farm life is back-breaking, draining on health and income. The struggles were more than your father wanted you to face. He wanted you to be happy and healthy and financially sound."

"Then why didn't he tell me that instead of pushing me away? We were close when I was a boy, but once he saw me play ball, he traded in his father hat for full-time coaching job. I didn't want another coach; I wanted a father."

Tears filled her eyes and overflowed. "I know. I tried to tell him that, but you know your father. The man was determined when he set his mind to something. And the night you came home and announced that you and Mary-Beth were done, your father decided to get you out of Sugar Maple before you changed your mind. Everyone saw the way you two looked at each other. And when you mentioned returning here after college, it did something to your father. He made it his mission to never allow you to live his life."

"Was it that bad of a life for him?" Tanner's chest ached, as if Gobbles rolled over him.

"No, he loved you boys. He just wanted more for you."

Tears streamed down her tan, farm-worn face, and he saw her exhaustion.

"Hawk and I would've gladly returned and worked the farm alongside him as a family."

She offered a faint smile. "I know. That's why I went along with the lie for a time. I thought you needed to know what was out there before you stayed here. This is all you ever knew. I wanted you to know the options you had beyond this farm."

"I would've gone to college while Hawk helped, and then he would've gone after I returned. We were a family. That's how I was raised." He released her hand and rubbed his temples, trying to see the other side of this betrayal. "Wait. You said in the beginning. Why didn't you tell us later?"

"Because I was overruled."

"You were bullied by Pops, you mean." Tanner fisted his hands; he'd vowed a long time ago never to be such a brute as his father. Sure, he was loving, but he could be all alpha with no room to listen to someone else.

"No. Not just your dad." Her voice wavered, as if she'd betrayed more than just Tanner and Mary-Beth.

"What are you saying, Mom?"

Mary-Beth, who'd sat quietly all this time allowing them to speak, sat forward. "It wasn't just your family. It was mine too. They all conspired against us. We never had a chance."

CHAPTER FIFTEEN

MARY-BETH'S MOUTH went cotton dry. "My parents... They instigated this entire thing, didn't they?"

Tanner looked between them. "Is that true?"

Mrs. McCadden nodded. "The night that you two fought, Mary-Beth's mother called with the idea of keeping you both apart. I told her and your father that was ridiculous and it would never work. But they insisted. And I'm afraid you know what happened after that. They'd been right. One lie, and you two never spoke again. You never chased after each other. Maybe I'd read too many romance novels or watched too many romantic comedies, but I'd expected you both to return, looking for the other one. I'd decided I'd confess the truth when you did, but it never happened."

Tanner gripped the arm of the chair. He took in three deep breaths, and Mary-Beth knew he was struggling with his temper.

Her bracelets felt like cuffs restraining her to her past, so she ripped them off and tossed them into the chair behind her. "So, this was all my mother's idea?"

"I'm not saying that. She came up with the idea to take your cell phone—"

"The one I thought was stolen?" A zap of realization shot through her like a bullet through bone.

Mrs. McCadden didn't even respond to the question. Instead she continued as if the trap door had opened and she had no choice but to fall through. "And they told you to leave town to look at your college dorm so that you two wouldn't run into each other that day."

"How could you do this, Mother?" Tanner shot up and paced, running his hand through his thick hair. "How could any of you do that to us? I thought you loved us."

"I do." His Mom reached for him, but he backed away.

Mary-Beth swiped tears from her eyes before they spilled out. "So, you tried to convince the others to tell us the truth?"

"Yes, I realized after you left how much it broke my son. And that's when I saw that he really loved you. The kind of love that molds and shapes a person's life. I wanted to run after you both and tell you the truth, but your mother and Tanner's father wouldn't allow it. They were convinced that they'd done the right thing. There was no arguing with them, but I was sure I'd be able to tell you the truth. I never had the chance, though." Her voice faded away.

"Why not?" Tanner said in a forced tone.

"Your father was diagnosed with cancer, and my life became caring for him. Everything else fell away around us. And when I saw how fast the farm deteriorated and how little I could do to save it, I realized that I was glad you were gone because I'd never want to see you work yourself into sickness and death. When I lost your father, it solidified my determination to never let you return to work the land, because I couldn't face losing you, too."

"But you did, Mother." He shot out the front door.

Mary-Beth felt for Mrs. McCadden. She'd lost so much. And in that moment, she knew she couldn't let her lose Tanner, too. "I'll go talk to him. What you did was wrong, but unlike my mother, I understand your motivation. I don't like it, but I understand it."

Mrs. McCadden stood, wavering a little, so Mary-Beth reached out for her. "Don't judge your mother too harshly. Talk to her. She had her reasons, too."

A gurgle of acid rose in Mary-Beth's throat. "What could those be?"

She'd only known her mother as a stranger all these years. A woman who came home after dinner and left before breakfast.

Mary-Beth had felt so guilty leaving Andy behind to be alone in that house, but he'd had football and his friends eventually. Unlike Tanner, she'd come home every chance she had to be with Andy. And now, she was making up for her own abandonment of her little brother for those four years.

"It isn't my place to say. Talk to her, though."

Mary-Beth chuckled. "Sure, because she's always willing to speak with me for more than five minutes."

"Make her talk to you. Don't let this ruin your relationship with your mother forever."

Mary-Beth heard the fear in Mrs. McCadden's voice. She couldn't let Tanner turn his back forever on his mother. She'd made a mistake, and it would take time, but it could be repaired.

It was different with her own mother. She headed to the door, mumbling, "What relationship?"

Outside, she spotted Stella in her greasy overalls, and her

friend snarled, "Tell that man he can never touch Gobbles again when I'm done."

"It wasn't his fault; he was sent away," Mary-Beth snapped.

"Whoa, which one of your bolts rusted today?" Stella tried to tease and cheer her up, but Mary-Beth fumed at the realization of the conspiracy that drove Tanner and her apart.

"Did you know?" Mary-Beth shouted more than spoke.

The rest of the Fabulous Five and Ms. Horton abandoned their individual chores and huddled around her.

"What's going on?" Ms. Horton asked.

Mary-Beth took in a stuttered breath. "You. If anyone knew about this, you did."

Ms. Horton caressed her hair like she was still a child.

Mary-Beth lifted her chin. "Tell me, did you know about the conspiracy to keep Tanner and me apart all this time?"

Jackie uncharacteristically gasped. Carissa grabbed Mary-Beth's bare wrist. Felicia narrowed her gaze at Ms. Horton.

"Tell me," Mary-Beth demanded.

Ms. Horton dropped her hand to her side and lifted her chin. "Not until you both returned. Mrs. McCadden confided in me after Tanner came home. She thought you two might just work things out and you'd be happy, but I urged her to tell you the truth. You both deserve that."

Jackie took Mary-Beth's hand. "What can I do?"

Carissa held tight to her. "I'm so sorry. If I had known..."

It was true, her friends would've told her. "I'm sorry for accusing you. I should've known none of you would keep a secret like that from me. It's just that..." Her voice faded away, and she wasn't sure what else to say.

"If your only family lied to you, who can you trust? We understand," Felicia offered in her diplomatic way.

Stella pushed up her sleeves. "Tell me who to take care of, and it's done."

Mary-Beth laughed. It broke her fog of hatred and let her realize she wasn't the only one harmed in all of this.

The girls surrounded her, hugging her tightly in the middle, but there was no comfort in it. Still, it was better than what Tanner had, which was nothing, no one to comfort him in this town.

"Nothing. There isn't anything any of you can do." She broke free and headed to find Tanner, the only person in the world who understood the way she felt at this moment.

CHAPTER SIXTEEN

TANNER FUMED. He knew the best place for him to be was expending his energy in a productive way. The way his father had taught him. At that thought, he picked up the pitchfork and impaled the hay. Luckily, the work crew on the roof had knocked off already, so he found the silent refuge he'd hoped for.

The sound of footsteps crunching hay warned Tanner that someone had entered the barn, but he didn't look up. He needed space before facing his mom again.

"In a strange way, I get your mom." Mary-Beth's voice was soothing, but her words were jagged and rough. "She wanted to save you from a hard life. It was wrong how she did it, but I understand. Your mom loves you."

He shoved the tines into the hay once more. "How can you say that?"

"Because she looked guilty and remorseful. I know she wished things were different. Trust me, my mother was the instigator. Don't you remember how she tried to control me yet was never around to enforce her demands?"

He rummaged through memories and snagged an incident from their past. "You mean when she thought you should wear the blue dress to prom, but you wanted to wear the red?"

"Yep, she took the red dress and hid it so that I couldn't wear it."

A picture of Mary-Beth standing at the bottom of her steps on prom night stuttered in his head. "You showed her, though. You cut that blue dress to barely permissible in public." He laughed, tossed the pitchfork into the hay, and faced the only woman he'd ever loved. The way he saw her was different, the resentment gone, and he could see the girl he once thought broke every rule with finesse but managed to always avoid trouble. "I thought your mother was going to have a stroke when she saw you."

"But the red dress reappeared." She winked, a sexy, grown-up wink that made his heart double tap. The woman who stood in front of him was no longer the girl from his past. Who was she? Had she changed? Of course. Hadn't they all?

"We need to talk, uninterrupted," Mary-Beth announced in a way that told him she had changed. She had grown into an independent person who didn't need him to take care of her.

He quirked his head toward the ladder. "Remember the hay loft?"

She blushed but shot past him and up the rungs to a more private area of the farm. A place where he could see and hear others while they were cloaked in wood and hay. His body awakened the way it would with any private moment with a woman, but this wasn't a woman he'd met in a bar or some football groupie... This was Mary-Beth Richards. A woman who would bring any man to his knees for a chance at one kiss. And she could kiss. The kind that ruined all other kisses in life.

He took his time climbing the rungs to focus on the importance of how he handled the situation. The knowledge that she hadn't abandoned him had opened a door he thought was locked forever.

The light filtered through the spaces between the wood planks that hadn't been repaired yet. The golden hues cascaded over them as if angels highlighted their time together as a gift. Yet, despite his desire and knowledge, something still warned him to pause a moment and take things slow. To get to know Mary-Beth as she was now, not how she was then.

And then a poisonous thought shot through him. What if she had someone else in her life? What if she didn't want the same thing? He settled by her side in a pile of hay like they were in high school.

"I know you're upset, so if you need time to think, we can sit for a while. It's just that I needed to be with someone who understood how I felt, and for once, that wasn't my friends. It's you," she said in a haunting tone.

He picked up a piece of hay and ran it through his fingers. "I know what you mean. This is so messed up. Where do we even start?" He knew where he wanted to start, yet part of him didn't want to know. For one day, he wanted to believe Mary-Beth was his again.

"Why don't we start with our fight? It was the trigger to the massacre of our relationship." She sounded wounded and lonely, which made him want to scoop her up into his lap and show her how much he'd missed her all these years.

"It was so long ago." He shot her a sideways glance and knew he wanted to connect with her and, if this was what made her feel closer to him, then he would open that door. "To be honest, I've spent so long trying to forget that day."

She reached out toward him but then dropped her hand to her lap. "I know what you mean."

What was she thinking? He wanted to know every thought in her head.

He returned to studying the hay in his hand. "When my father first told me about the full ride to Notre Dame, I snorted at him. I mean, literally. It was insane. First of all, there was no way it could be true. Small-town high school player getting a full ride to a top school?"

"I never had a doubt you were good enough," she said in a shallow voice, as if that fact tormented her.

"But I wanted to go to UT, despite the opportunity. It was our plan. We had it all set."

"You couldn't pass up Notre Dame. I know that now. I wasn't fair that night. It's just that you shocked me. And then my mother told me you would always choose football over me."

"No, I wouldn't have, but my father convinced me that if you really loved me, you'd support me and we'd figure out how to get you to Notre Dame with me or make a long-distance relationship work until we got through college."

"I couldn't afford that, and I went on partial scholarship to UT, so I only had to take out loans for fees, room and board, and a few extra classes that weren't covered. There's no way it would've worked out with me following you to Notre Dame. And I knew I had to let you go. You'd resent me if I held you back."

"I never would've resented you."

"You say that, but you don't know. We never had the chance to find out. I don't want to add fuel to this bonfire of lies, but did your parents ever tell you that I came back to find you after I returned from my dorm? I told them that I wanted to speak to you, and I gave them my new cell number, and I waited for your call."

"Why didn't you call me? You had my number."

"I did."

"No, you didn't."

She sighed. "It was a couple of weeks after you'd left for school. You'd come back to pick up some stuff for your dorm. Felicia told me you were here, so I called. Your father answered your phone."

"He didn't tell me." His chest burned with animosity toward the man he'd once worshiped as a boy.

She looked at him with misty eyes. "I realize that now, but at the time, he told me you'd moved on with a new girl and I would only torture myself if I tried to hang on to you. That you were meant for a big life, and I was a small-town girl."

Tanner tossed the hay down and grabbed her hand, willing her to listen. "Never. I wanted you by my side, but I was told I was being unfair. That you'd moved on." He groaned and closed his eyes for a moment. "Lies. So many lies."

She rested her head back against the wall and looked up at the roof, as if searching for answers. "Tell me, have you had a good life? Have you achieved what you wanted in your career? You're an assistant coach at a major university. That's a big deal."

"Not head coach, which is what I thought I'd be by now, but there are so many politics, and you have to put in your time to achieve that position. I'm still younger than the youngest head coach ever. Still, yes, I've had a good life. Just not the one I would've chosen."

Mary-Beth's phone rang, and she stood, slid it from her pocket, and checked the screen. "I'm so sorry. I wouldn't answer this, but it's the shop."

"Go ahead. I'm not going anywhere this time."

She offered a sad smile, and he longed to see that shine and spunk she'd once possessed.

"Hello? Everything okay?" She gasped. "Oh no. I forgot about the date. I'll call him." She glanced at Tanner with wide eyes and stepped away, lowering her voice. "He's there already? Okay, tell him I'm on my way." She hung up and held the phone tight when she faced him. "I'm sorry. I have to go."

"I heard. Date, huh?" He shoved from the ground, wanting to tell her she wasn't going, but he'd never be his father. Not the man who bullied his mother into keeping secrets.

"I—"

"Don't. It's fine. I understand. We can speak more later." He stood there, longing to pull her into his arms and refuse her the opportunity to ever see another man again, but that wouldn't be the answer. She had to choose. He only hoped this time, she would choose him.

CHAPTER SEVENTEEN

MARY-BETH RACED to the coffee shop, but she left her heart back at the farm. How could she go out with Seth when she'd discovered the man she loved hadn't abandoned her like she'd thought? She dialed Felicia before she even reached the bridge, knowing Ms. Negotiator would be the best at this kind of advice.

"You all right?" Felicia asked without even a greeting.

"Yes, but I need some advice. You remember Seth, the guy I had a date with the other night that I canceled?"

"Yes."

"He's at Maple Grounds, waiting for me for our date tonight. I've already canceled on him twice. It wouldn't be right to ditch him. Not again. Right? I mean, the poor guy is so nice and understanding. He deserves better than how I've treated him. But is it right to string him along when I know he isn't the right guy for me?"

"Take a breath," Felicia ordered. "How do you know Seth isn't the right guy for you? You found out your ex-boyfriend's back, but what do you really know about the grown-up

Tanner? Is he married? Does he have a girlfriend? Will he ever return to Sugar Maple for good? Did he tell you that he still loves you?"

Her words weren't easy to digest and more direct than a normal Felicia speech. "I'm not sure. No."

"Then why not go on the date? You have nothing to lose. If you go out and you decide that Seth isn't right for you, then fine, but you've only been out twice, and you said you liked him before Tanner waltzed back into town. If you cancel on Seth this time, I have it on good authority that he won't ask again."

She pulled to the corner and spotted Seth with flowers in hand, standing near the register. Geesh, she felt like a shmuck.

"All I'm saying is you should only treat Seth the way you would want to be treated. And that you shouldn't jump to conclusions without knowing all the information. Besides, do you really want Jackie to win the bet?"

Mary-Beth pulled into a parking space in back and knew she didn't have a choice. Not with Seth already here. Besides, Felicia had a point. Mary-Beth would never want to admit Jackie was right and have to wear those darn shoes in public. "I've got to go. Thanks."

"You know we love you. Good luck."

Mary-Beth ended the call and raced upstairs to change into a dress and boots then flew down with no more than a hair fluff and lipstick. Serena eyed her with a disapproving glower. "Sorry. And thanks for covering for me."

Serena didn't respond. Something told Mary-Beth this girl was upset about more than covering for her, but that was a problem she'd have to handle later.

She offered Seth a friendly smile at the entrance to the

customer area. "Hi. I'm so sorry I'm late. The wedding plans for Ms. Horton are all-consuming these days."

He kissed her cheek and handed her the flowers.

"You didn't have to." She acted like she sniffed them but was careful not to breathe in, since she was allergic to chrysanthemums. "Thank you. They're beautiful. Let me go put these in water, and then we can go."

She held them at arm's length and took them to her office but knew they couldn't stay there or her eyes would swell shut by morning. "Hey, Serena," she called out in a whispered tone.

"Yes?" Serena eyed the flowers down the end of her nose.

"I hate to ask this, but would you take these home with you? I'm allergic, and I don't want to hurt Seth's feelings."

She half smiled. "Yeah, sure. Those are my favorite."

"Thanks so much. You sure you're good with closing tonight? I know it's our late night with the two book clubs coming."

"I'll be fine."

"Thanks. I owe you big-time."

Mary-Beth returned to Seth and followed him out to his expensive car, where he opened her door and tucked her inside. He was a gentleman for sure. Maybe Felicia was right and she needed to give the man a chance. Once he settled into the driver's seat, she asked him, "So how was your day at work?"

"Fair. Still plugging through the paperwork for the Taiwan deal; I'll be flying out for meetings next week."

"Right, you'll be gone again." Why did that make her happy more than upset?

"Yes, but once the deal is done, I'll be back," he offered, taking her hand and kissing her knuckles. It felt foreign, wrong…despite that being his go-to move on all their dates. Maybe that was the problem. It felt rehearsed, planned.

He released her so he could navigate through the parking lot to find a spot, and she held tight to her handbag like a date-advancement shield.

"I thought we could have dinner and then maybe have a drink at my place."

His words were like tiny insects shot under her skin—itchy and frightening. They'd never been alone before. "That sounds good, but I'm afraid I'll need to get back to the shop to help close up tonight. It's Serena's first time by herself, so she might need some help." There, that was a viable excuse. She needed more time to figure things out. Seth was handsome, hardworking—even if she found his job boring—and a gentleman. A catch for any woman. That's why she was going on a third date with him.

He opened the door and offered his arm to escort her inside. "I hope you like steak, since this is the only place in Sugar Maple I could find that might provide us a little time away from everyone you know deciding to chat while we eat."

"Right. I forgot you're not used to small-town living." She took his arm and followed him inside to the dimly lit romantic steakhouse that all men took their girls to for a real date in town. No doubt Tanner would hear of it by morning.

"I don't think small-town life is for me. I mean, of course, I lived here for part of high school, and I can live here part-time since I travel so much, so don't worry, I won't run off on you." He pulled out her chair and then settled into his own seat.

Run off on me? Tanner hadn't run off on her. He'd been sent away. She shook off the thought.

"Are you cold? You can have my coat."

"No, I'm good. But thanks." She watched him align the fork with the knife. "So, you're not meant for small-town life."

He grinned. "No, not really. But as I said, I understand you have a business here for now, so I have no problem residing here."

"For how long?" she asked, realizing this wasn't just about Tanner being in town. This was about if Seth was right for her.

"I don't know. However long it takes." He placed the napkin on his lap and summoned the waiter over to order a bottle of wine. Which he did with perfect pronunciation and authority. And she had no clue what he'd ordered.

When the waiter left, she returned to their discussion, eager to learn more. "How long what takes?"

He shifted in his seat. "All I mean is, once you get some more help at your shop, you'll probably want to go on trips with me. See the world, right? I mean, who wouldn't? And then, maybe we'll spend extra time in certain areas of the world. You'll love London and Paris."

"I love Sugar Maple," she said flatly.

The waiter returned and poured a smidgen of wine in the bottom of the glass. Seth swirled it, smelled it, swirled it again, and then took a sip, swished, swallowed. Then he finally held his glass up with a slight nod of approval. "I like it here, too. That's why I'm here."

She shook her head, realizing this man hoped to sweep her off her feet and show her the world. This guy was meant for Jackie, not her. "Seth, I need to tell you something."

He waited for the server to pour their glasses and walk away. "Sounds serious." He eyed her glass, as if waiting for her approval, so she drank a gulp and set it down to appease him. The lingering taste of black cherry remained.

"You're a nice guy, but we're not right for each other."

His face morphed from friendly to agitated. "How would you know that? It's only our third date."

"I usually know by date three. Trust me."

"That's not an answer."

"Because I'm a Sugar Maple girl. I'm not meant for Paris and London or anywhere else. Sure, I might travel to those places someday, but I'll never move away from here. I'm a small-town girl with small-town dreams. I'm sure that sounds boring to you, but that's me."

He looked at her as if she were Russian trying to speak French. "That's only because you haven't been away from here before. Once you do, you'll see what I have to offer."

The server returned, but Seth waved him away.

She swirled the glass, trying to appear sophisticated, but some sloshed out, splattering burgundy across the white linen. "I know what you have to offer, but it isn't what I want."

"This is about that boy Tanner, the one from high school, the star football player who washed out in college."

His words caused her muscles to tighten. "He was injured."

Seth shook his head. "I see now."

"You see what?"

"You're still in love with Tanner McCadden. And he's going to break your heart. Again."

CHAPTER EIGHTEEN

TANNER WORKED until the dark of night drove him inside. Sleeping seemed unattainable, so he set up some lanterns and lights in the barn and took apart the old tractor engine.

The horses neighed at him, as if he disrupted their peace with hammering and foul words he shouted when the wrench slipped and cut his hand. The slam of the front door of the house warned Tanner his mother was about to invade his hideout.

Footsteps crunched across the leaves, and her lantern shone into the barn behind him. "Can't sleep? Do you want me to make you some warm milk?"

"I'm not twelve," he snapped, but even with how he felt about her lies, he knew better than to speak to his mom that way. "Sorry."

"I understand, son. I'd be upset, too. I wish I could turn back time and change everything, but I can't. I hope you can someday find it in your heart to forgive us."

"You, yes. Father, never," he said in a tone that caused a coldness to engulf the room.

She remained at the edge of the front stall, as if in fear he'd send her away if she came too close. "Hon, you have it wrong. Your father loved you more than anything. Don't hate him. He made mistakes, but anything and everything he did was what he believed to be best for you."

He shot up and looked at her. "Why are you defending him? He always bullied you into doing what he wanted."

"That's not true." She narrowed her gaze at him, but he resumed work, wiping the dirt and grime away.

"Then explain why you never went to New York City to see a Broadway show?"

"We couldn't afford it or the time away. A farm doesn't work itself." She scooted closer. "Can't you see, that's why we wanted more for you. We knew what it was like to sacrifice your dreams to survive."

"But you could afford to send me to football camp in Nashville my junior year."

"That's different."

"Why?"

"Because we wanted to help you have a start in life, and there weren't many opportunities for you here. I didn't want either of you to have to go into the military to make it, but that's what Hawk ended up doing because we couldn't pay for his room and board at UT."

"He always wanted to be a marine. That was *his* dream." Tanner placed the fuel filter on the ground and picked up the starter motor.

"Yes, but we wanted him to have options. All I'm trying to say is that your father wanted you both to have a better future."

Tanner didn't know if it was his exhaustion or his mom convincing him that they got a free pass for lying because they tried to allegedly give him and his brother a better life. No, he wouldn't let it go that easily. This had been life changing. "But when he was sick, why didn't you call me then?"

"Your father didn't want to bring you home. He thought he could beat it, and he did." Her voice cracked, and he couldn't take it anymore. He rose and put a comforting arm around her. "We didn't know his heart would fail, or I would have called you home to say goodbye. I promise."

"I believe you, but now I don't get to have it out with him. I feel guilty being mad when he isn't here to defend himself, which makes me feel more frustrated." He squeezed his mom to his side. "I'm so sorry you went through all of this alone. Again, another instance of Pops bullying you."

"He didn't bully me. I chose not to contact you. It was as much my decision as his."

"I don't believe that." Tanner leaned away enough to see her. "You wouldn't do that."

"I would, because I'm selfish and I wanted to have some alone time with your father before he died. I'd intended on telling you, but then we were told that he'd beaten cancer, so there was no reason to." She bowed her head in obvious shame. "Again, it was my decision and my fault you didn't get to say goodbye."

Tanner sat there, unsure what to do next. He eyed the darkness outside and couldn't help but think about Mary-Beth on a date with Seth. He'd gone off and done well for himself since high school. He'd been a couple grades above them, so Tanner never really knew the guy except he'd lived in Sugar Maple for two years and then left.

"Have you told her you still love her?" his mom asked.

He returned to cleaning the engine. "Who?"

"Don't be coy. It doesn't suit you."

"Don't know how I feel, and I can't figure it out because she's on a date with someone else." He grinded his teeth, trying to keep from raising his voice and telling his mom it was her fault that they were apart for so long.

"Are you going to let her slip away again?"

She had some nerve, asking him such a question.

"I never let her slip away." He held tight to the cold piece of metal.

She stood over him, looking down. "Why didn't you ever return after your injury?"

"You know why. Father told me not to come home, to stay and finish my degree."

"No, that's not why. I was there when he called you. I heard him. He asked you what you were going to do, and you said finish college. That's when he said good for you because there is no life here for you."

Tanner thought back to that night when he'd come out of knee surgery groggy, afraid, confused, and alone. He'd known his parents couldn't afford to fly there to see him. He'd planned to convalesce back at the farm, but he'd decided he couldn't. "Because I didn't want to return a failure. To see Mary-Beth succeed while I failed."

The realization stole his breath. His lungs tightened.

His mom didn't say another word. She only disappeared from the barn, leaving him with his thoughts. It didn't matter how she'd spun it; they'd been the catalyst that ended his relationship with Mary-Beth, but he was the one who never came back to fight for her. How could he? He hadn't felt worthy after his accident. He'd slipped away from the world. If it hadn't been for his football coach arranging his tuition through a scholarship fund, Tanner would've been completely lost.

But if he had returned home, what would've happened? Back then the people of Sugar Maple thought he was invincible and worshiped him. He wasn't strong enough to face the fact he'd let everyone down, and that fear had kept him away for too long. But now there was nothing to tear him from Sugar Maple, the farm, his mom, or Mary-Beth, so he needed to fight for what he wanted. And he wanted Mary-Beth.

CHAPTER NINETEEN

JACKIE STOOD at the back entrance to Maple Grounds with the bedazzled, beguiling, begrudgingly-have-to-wear-them darn shoes.

"How'd you get those?"

Jackie slid the spare key to Mary-Beth's apartment out of her pocket.

"That's supposed to be for emergencies only."

"I'd call this a friend-urgency. You ditched Seth last night on date three. I'm trying to help you realize you're hung up on Puff the Magic Jock."

Mary-Beth would never renege on a bet, so she snatched the shoes from Jackie. "Fine, but I'll get even. Just wait, I'll find a way to get you on a date."

Jackie swirled with her auburn hair whipping like a witch's broom, and she marched out with only a comment left behind. "Never going to beat me."

The morning rush kept Mary-Beth busy, but in the midmorning lull, she struggled to keep her focus on her work. It didn't help that every time she rounded the counter and people saw the shoes, they'd giggle. No doubt Jackie had notified the gossip line. She went through billing and paying vendors, but she made three errors and had to start over. After making herself a cup of coffee, she settled at the bistro table at the front window so she could watch the goings on as she worked. Those darn sparkly pink tennis shoes were distracting on her feet. A bet was a bet, though.

Last night had been a potential disaster, but Seth had come to see her point easy enough. The man was wealthy, successful, and had political aspirations in life. He needed a corporate woman who loved to live out of a suitcase. That was not her.

Now there was nothing that stood in her way of being with Tanner. Was there? Something held her back, though. She'd been waiting ten years for this opportunity. Why wasn't she running after him to rekindle their once epic love?

The bell jingled, and in came the elders with all their wonderful distractions. "Hey, Davey. How's it going today?"

He shuffled to his favorite spot and settled in for a long visit with Ms. Gina, Ms. Melba, and Felicia's mom, Mrs. Hughes, at his side.

"I'm not dead, so it's a good day." He pointed at her shoes. "Not so good for you, though."

Mrs. Hughes swatted him in the arm. "Don't listen to him. He's still young at heart and dances better than any man I've ever known."

"I didn't expect y'all today. It's not Wednesday." Mary-Beth snagged her empty mug and waited for them all to sit.

"We thought we'd come check on you since we heard all about your date last night and you discovering that awful truth about the parents' conspiracy."

"How'd you guys know all this stuff before anyone else?"

"We founded and run this town. Nothing gets by us," Davey said with a hint of street kid accent.

"Doesn't sound like I could have much to share. You know it all." She set to work making their beverages.

To Mary-Beth's surprise, Davey followed her into the back, leaving the ladies behind. Shuffling his feet, he looked anywhere but at her until Mary-Beth touched his arm gently

"I need yer opinion," he mumbled still looking at his feet.

"Sure. What's up?"

He held out a small box. "It's been fifty or so years in the making, but I hope she likes it."

Mary-Beth wiped her hands on her towel and opened the lid to find a diamond ring inside. "Wow! Which one of the lucky ladies?" she teased.

"This player's gonna be off the market. I'll be a one-woman kind of man. I've had that ring all these years, you know. We were supposed to get married when we were seventeen, but things happened to break us up. Point is, we finally found our way back to each other. That's what happens when you truly love someone."

Mary-Beth handed the ring back to him. "Why do I get the hint you're trying to tell me something?"

Davey looked behind him, as if he worried he'd get busted with the ring, but then he slid it into his pocket and whispered conspiratorially, "You know what I'm saying. That boy Tanner and you were made to be together. Go get your man. Don't wait fifty years. Trust me." He scooted out of the kitchen before she had a chance to say anything else.

No way she'd wait fifty years, but she'd barely been able to digest all the information in the last twelve hours. Maybe after work she'd go speak to him again. They'd be at football practice until five, but she could find him at the farm after she closed shop at seven.

The door bell jingled, so she poked her head out to find Tanner standing in the center of the shop holding wildflowers. She removed her apron and walked out to greet him. "What's this?"

"Flowers for you."

She took in a deep breath and enjoyed the farm aroma in her shop. "Thank you. They're beautiful."

He smiled but shifted his feet nervously. "I chose to pick them instead of purchase them in the square, since all of them had chrysanthemums in them. And I know you're—"

"Allergic. You remembered." Her heart fluttered at the idea that he knew her so well.

"Of course." He spied her shoes and laughed. "I see the rumors are true."

She twisted her heel up to show him the side in its complete gaudy glory.

"To me they are the most beautiful shoes I've ever seen since they mean you're unattached at the moment." He fidgeted. Was the confident Tanner nervous? "I came to see if you'd like to go on a date tonight. If you don't already have plans."

"That's my boy," Davey cheered from behind them.

Mary-Beth looked down at the flowers and then back at Tanner. Butterflies, bees, and all other insects in the night buzzed in her belly. "I think I'd like that. Should I meet you at the farm?"

"No, I'll pick you up here after the shop closes. Seven thirty sound good?"

"Sounds perfect. How should I dress?" she asked, not sure

where he was taking her, but she hoped it wasn't some stuffy restaurant.

"What you're wearing is fine. No need to dress up. Not for me. I like you just the way you are." He leaned in and kissed her on the cheek, sending a warm flush down her neck.

"That's my boy," Davey repeated. He smacked the table for extra emphasis this time. "I taught him all those moves, you know."

Mary-Beth ignored him and watched Tanner strut out the door, mount his bike, and speed out of town. This time, she only hoped he'd return.

She went to work preparing beverages for the elders and then attempted to concentrate on the books again, but her mind kept wondering to what ifs and what could be. After seeing the elders out, she abandoned the financial stuff and decided to create new coffee blends and flavors. By late afternoon, she had two trays full of trial shots for customers.

Stella and Knox walked in with laptop in hand, and that's when she remembered the planning for the upcoming show. She quickly whipped up something for them both and sat down with them. "Oh wait." She shot up and grabbed the tray of samples. "Before you dig into your drinks, try these. I'm looking for a new signature drink for the wedding." She placed samples in front of each of them. "These are all fall themed. Taste them and tell me if you like any of them and which is the best."

Stella picked one up, took a shot like a bad whiskey, and then slammed it down on the table. "It's good."

Knox picked one up and sipped it like fine, aged wine. "Mmm, I like this one. It's good to know the Coffee Whisperer can still...whisper."

Could she though? Could she claim the title when she couldn't coffee whisper Tanner?

He set it down and sipped the other samples and then pointed at the second from the left. "This one. It's the winner."

Stella tried it. "He's right. It's a blend of Ms. Horton and Mr. Strickland with a dash of fall. Perfect."

Mary-Beth pushed the tray aside and faced her friend. "I'm glad I can still get it right for someone."

Knox cleared his throat and opened his laptop. "We should work on the concept for the show. I was thinking—"

"That now isn't a good time." Stella nudged the laptop away.

"I'll do whatever you say to make your segment great. Just let me know." Mary-Beth placed the samples back onto the tray and fled to her office.

Stella followed before Mary-Beth could even set the tray down. "Are you okay?"

"No. I can't do it."

"Can't do what?" Stella edged into the room but kept her distance.

"Be on Knox's show."

"Why not?" Stella asked.

"Even if I wanted to, I can't."

"Why not?" Stella asked, nudging a little closer.

Mary-Beth struggled with the reality of her failure. "Because the Coffee Whisperer still can't whisper her ex."

CHAPTER TWENTY

TANNER SHOWERED in the high school locker room and raced out the door.

The players whistled at him. "Coach has a hot date with Andy's sister."

Andy bolted forward, but two of his friends held him back.

"Save it for the field, boys. The game's only a week away." Tanner strutted out, ignoring Andy's comment from behind about him not hurting his sister. It was sweet that Andy worried wanted to protect her and Tanner understood and respected him for it, but Tanner needed to pursue how he felt about Mary-Beth. Besides Andy had nothing to worry about because Tanner would never hurt her.

Tanner got on his bike and hoped he'd get Mary-Beth and make their escape before Andy made it back to the coffee shop. The last thing they needed was another person inserting themselves into …whatever they were. His hands hurt from gripping the handles so tight. When was the last time he was so nervous to pick up a girl? Never.

The coffee shop was closed with only dim lighting inside.

He knocked on the door, and Mary-Beth appeared from the back office. She looked radiant, as if she'd stepped out in a ballgown, high heels, and an updo instead of a sweater, jeans, boots, and of course, her jewelry.

He fought to catch his breath at the sight before she opened the door for him. He'd been planning this date all day, and he wanted it to be perfect. "You ready?"

"Yes." She grabbed her bag from the table and locked up, despite her shaking hands trying to get the key into the lock. Was she as nervous as he was for their first time being together in a decade?

"I hope you don't mind riding on my motorcycle," he said nervously, hoping she wouldn't since it was his only means of transportation. He could've rented a car, but this would force them closer on the bike than they'd have been in bucket seats.

"It's been a while, but we had fun on them when we were younger." She stepped up to the bike, and he gently slid the helmet over her head, careful not to snag her earrings.

"Ready?"

"Sure." She looked adorable with the helmet on and her hair fluffed around her face. He couldn't wait to mount the bike, because that meant she'd have her arms around him the way she had when they were teenagers. He started the engine and made sure Mary-Beth was snug behind him.

"Hold on."

She slid her hands around him, clasping them at his front and causing a heat to radiate through his body.

They flew through town and headed to the trail between the farm and where Mary-Beth grew up. To his surprise, the old dirt road had grown over. He hadn't checked from this direction since he'd walked from the farm earlier. Darn. He'd thought he'd checked and planned every detail so well. He stopped and removed his helmet, dismounting the bike. "Sorry, we'll have to walk from here."

She took off her helmet with a smile. "Taking me to our old stomping grounds to dredge up old memories?"

He hesitated, making sure he hadn't miscalculated his play. "I can take you to a restaurant instead if you prefer."

"No, no fancy restaurants, please," she said with such conviction, he gained confidence in his plan.

"Good, then come with me." He offered his hand. "Stay close. I only have the one flashlight." He flicked on the light, and they walked side-by-side when the trees didn't force them into single file. The temperature dropped as they moved farther into the woods, and he worried Mary-Beth was too cold, so he took off his jacket and wrapped it around her.

He managed to find the camp and lit the pre-made fire quickly.

"I can't believe this is still here." She looked up at the old tree house. He'd managed to do some repair work on it earlier —not enough to make it perfect but safe enough to enter if they wished.

"It is. I guess we make a good team." He settled her onto a blanket laid out next to the picnic basket and then covered her with the other and snuggled in by her side. Between the campfire, the blankets, and the body heat, they'd be warm enough.

"Wow, what's all this?" She pointed to the picnic basket.

"I made our favorite food. Hopefully, it's as good as what my mother used to make for us. I did have to ask her what kind of jelly she always used when we were kids under the guise that I was craving one." He winked.

"So, you two are speaking. That's good." She looked down

at her covered feet stretched out in front of her. He hated the sadness that showed in the way her bottom lip tightened.

"And your mother? Are you speaking with her?" he asked.

Mary-Beth opened the picnic basket and looked inside. "No, not yet. I wasn't ready. Your mother's easy to forgive."

"I hope you do. Trust me when I say it feels better to hash it out. I don't have the opportunity to do so with my father, and I wish I could. Don't let things go too long without talking. You'll have regrets."

She looked at him as if for the first time, studying every inch of his face before she spoke again. "I'm sorry. I know that has to be tough."

For a moment, he thought they would fall into each other's arms and move forward, but she pulled away and removed the foil to unveil the peanut butter sandwiches, chips, and apple with a hearty laugh. "I can't believe you brought our camp food. We thought it was so cool when your mom would make us this and tell us to go play and we'd take it to the tree house to hide from Hawk so we could have some privacy." She bit into the apple, sending juice down her chin. He grabbed a napkin and caught the liquid before it dropped to the blanket. Any excuse to lean into her without making her pull away worked for him.

"You sure you don't want me to take you some place special?" he asked, worried this wasn't good enough to win her affection again.

"This is the most special place in the world. It was our place, and it feels good to be here again." She looked overhead. "Do you think we can fit inside?"

"I don't know, but we can try." He stood, careful to keep the blanket from the fire, and pulled down the rope ladder for her. "Do you think you can still climb?"

"Better than you."

She managed to make it to the top after he held the ladder still so it didn't swing. He had the same difficulty, but it was worth it when he reached the top and found that the flameless candles were still on. He'd set the scene before he'd left for football practice, in hopes it would stay lit long enough to get Mary-Beth here.

"Wow, this is beautiful. Look, our little table you made in scouts for us is still here. And the chair I made with your mom while you were at football practice." She spun around with her head quirked to one side so she fit.

He stayed on his knees with no hope of walking around. "Do you remember how we would come out here any time we needed a break from the world? We'd always say this was for just you and me."

"I remember." She scooted to the chair and knelt down. "Hey, I wonder if our tin box is still inside." She opened the secret compartment.

His breath caught. He knee-walked to her side, ignoring the shooting pain in his bad leg. "No. Don't open that."

She pulled the tin box out. "Why not? Scared there's a beetle inside?"

"That was only once, and I didn't know it was a beetle. It was dark, and the thing moved like a snake. It was some mutant creature." He reached for the tin box to take it from her, not sure if his letter still remained inside after all these years. How had he been so stupid? He'd been so excited to bring her out here and share a night alone that he hadn't thought to check.

"Relax, I'll protect you from any insects." She opened it, and inside sat his old, crinkled letter, dusty and dirty, but it had remained in its dismal resting place.

"Don't open that." He reached, but she pulled it away.

"Why, what is it?"

"My final note to you. The one I placed here when you'd left for the dorm. A letter I thought would've changed things between us." He saw it in her eyes that she had to open it and see.

And she did.

The dirty, tarnished old ring fell into the palm of her hand.

CHAPTER TWENTY-ONE

THE HANDWRITTEN LETTER nearly disintegrated in her hands, but the ring slipped through the tear in the paper before she could make anything out. The gold band with a diamond chip sat in her palm, and she analyzed it as if she'd never seen a ring before.

"I didn't have any money back then."

His words jolted her from her stupor.

"It's perfect. It's not that. Tanner... It's the most beautiful thing I've ever seen." Tears filled her eyes, but she swiped them away, wanting to see the letter he'd left for her. She lifted one of the candles and tried to make out the fading words. Love, will you, and marry was all she could read. Her hands trembled, as did her heart. "What did it say? I want to hear every word that you wrote me. Please tell me you remember."

He slid to her side and took both of her hands in his. "It said that I knew that I'd made a mistake leaving you behind and that I wanted you to come with me. I loved you, and I wanted to ask you to marry me."

His words were tarnished by the years and the realization that their parents had been right. He'd wanted that game more than anything, even more than her. "I'm glad I didn't get this all those years ago."

"What? Why?"

"Because our parents were right about one thing. I would've been a distraction from your dreams. You see, I never wanted to be your shadow. I wanted to find my own way, and with football and fame, I don't know if I could've handled it."

"Don't say that." Tanner held her hands in his. "You've just let them get into your head. Mary-Beth, you could never be my shadow. You shine too brightly. I've always admired the way you light up a room and how everyone wants to be close to you. The world loves you for you, not just because you can catch or throw a ball and score a touchdown."

"You were meant to be a star, Tanner. I'm sorry for what happened to you. I truly hope you've been happy as a coach."

"Yes, but I'll be happier here with you. I want to stay and run the farm and help with high school football. I don't mind hard work if it means that I get to have you back in my life." He took the ring and held it up to her. "This might be a little tarnished and dirty, but I assure you my feelings for you are not. I want you to keep this as a reminder of how much I've loved you over the years. How I never forgot about you, and someday, I hope to get you a real ring and we can be together without any family pulling us apart."

"I'd like that too, but Tanner, where do we go from here?" She wanted to launch into his arms and tell him how much she loved him and wanted to spend her life with him, but she'd suffered so many years filling the hole where her heart was that she couldn't risk herself again. Not without more confidence in who they were today.

"Can we pick up where we left off and pretend we were never torn apart?" He sounded winded and hopeful, but she couldn't give that to him.

"No. Because we're not the same people we once were." She fisted the ring and held it to her heart. "I loved this boy and trusted him with everything, and he broke me. The man you've become... I don't know him."

"Then get to know me. We'll date. I'll take you out to restaurants and walk you to work and do boyfriendly things."

She swiped more wayward tears and looked at a wide-eyed Tanner at her side. She'd never been able to deny him anything he wanted. But for now, she wouldn't give her hope and heart to him. Not yet. "I'd like that, except for the traditional dating. I'm hoping we can be ourselves. I've never been me around another man the way I was with you."

"I know what you're saying. There's no girl who I've ever been myself around. We grew up together, we knew each other, and I want to know you that way again. Give us a chance. Trust me with your heart. I promise not to break it this time."

She held out the ring to him, but he closed her fingers around it. "Keep it. Consider it a promise ring, and when you feel safe in my arms, then put it on your finger. Until then, I'll properly date you, and as good ole Davey would say, I'll *woo* you."

"Taking advice from Davey now?" She ran her thumb over the ring that promised him to her.

"Maybe." He shrugged with a boyish look that took her back to childhood.

"What other advice did he give you?" she asked.

"To kiss you," he said with a mischievous grin.

Part of her wanted to launch into his arms and kiss him for all the kisses they'd missed over the years, but would it be the same? It couldn't be. Her toes wouldn't curl, her pulse wouldn't race, the world wouldn't fade away around them. But she knew she needed to take a chance if she wanted to know what their future held. "Well, we wouldn't want to go against an elder's advice."

She didn't even have a chance to lean in before he cupped the back of her neck and claimed her mouth with passion that burned her insides, despite the cold air, and filled her body with want and need as she hadn't felt for years. But most of all, she felt safe in his arms, loved in his arms, cherished, and all she wanted was to be held all night and never be let go.

His thumb grazed her cheek, and he moved in closer, claiming her as his own. The passion was palpable. She knew one thing... He had missed her as much as she had yearned for him. And in that moment, she believed. Believed that he was really here to stay and wouldn't abandon her. They would never be torn apart again.

CHAPTER TWENTY-TWO

THE NEXT MORNING, the sun shone, the birds sang, and the air smelled fresh and clean. Tanner bolted down the stairs. "Hey, Mama. How's your morning?" The aroma of bacon and pancakes made his stomach growl.

"Who are you?" She smacked his hand with the spatula before he could steal a pancake.

He rubbed the sting from his knuckles. "What are you talking about?"

She turned the knob on the stove, and the flames flickered and then exploded into a dull burn. "I'm talking about the fact that you're not moping, angry, or carrying on about something. You're smiling. Did you whiten your teeth?"

"Mama, stop." He kissed her cheek, distracting her from one side while he grabbed one of the pancakes.

"I take it things went well last night with you and Mary-Beth." She poured batter into the pan with a sizzle.

"How did you know I saw her last night? I could've been hanging with some old friends." He took a gargantuan bite, consuming half the pancake. Rich, buttery sweet clouds mushed between his teeth. No one had ever made pancakes like his mom.

"In the tree house? I could see the fire burning out there."

He choked and coughed until he managed to speak again. "You knew about our top-secret tree house?"

"The one you built by stealing wood from the shed construction project?"

He poured a glass of milk and downed a few gulps before he could answer. "You knew that was us?"

"The two kids who giggled the entire time and dragged the large pieces, leaving a trail to your secret hideout. Um...yep."

"You never said anything."

"Neither did your father. He liked that you were having fun, and he liked Mary-Beth. He just wanted you to find your way before you committed to the rest of your life."

Her words made sense, but if they had understood how in love he and Mary-Beth had been, would they have done the same thing? "I bought a ring."

The spatula clanged against the pan and flipped out, clattering to the floor. "When?"

"When I came back to get my second load to drive up to Notre Dame." He gripped the glass tight and prayed that the next time he saw Mary-Beth, she'd be wearing the ring. "She found it last night." He bent down and picked up the spatula.

"What did she say?" Mom asked in her I-love-you-no-matter-what tone.

"That she was glad I hadn't proposed back then because she could never shine better than me and football. I told her she's always shined." Tanner shrugged. "That she wants to get to know the adult version of me."

"Sounds like a good idea." His mom rinsed off the spatula, the water sputtering and ringing in the old pipes. He didn't even care that it was one more thing that needed attention on the farm. The singing was like a welcome home call.

He leaned against the counter and crossed his arms over his chest. "What does that even mean? She knows me better than anyone. Next to you of course."

She flipped a pancake, plopped another one on top of the others, and poured the last of the batter onto the griddle. "You both have changed over the years. You're different people now. There's no reason to rush into anything. Right?"

"No, I guess not." He grabbed a plate and reached for another pancake but got slapped again. "What? I have a plate."

"Yes, but your guest isn't here yet."

A warning signal flashed like the neon sign in his head. "What guest?"

"The one coming up the drive now."

He tensed and listened. Sure enough, gravel crunched, so he rushed to the front window of the parlor to peer out in time to see Mary-Beth get out of her car and walk up the front steps with coffee cups in a Styrofoam cup holder. Tanner's breath came in rapid puffs. He took a moment to calm himself then opened the door. "Good morning, beautiful."

"Morning." She removed a cup and passed it to him. "Try this."

His excitement deflated at the sight of her bare finger. She must have noticed, because when he took the cup, she reached for a chain around her neck and the ring swung back and forth from it. "I'll keep it by my heart."

"I can live with that, for now." He was so sure she was the one and only one, and now that he'd returned there would be nothing that could come between them, so he only needed to be patient until she could see that for herself. Until she trusted that they would make it through lies and future plans this time.

He ushered her inside and closed the door to avoid any falling leaves swooping inside and onto his mom's floor. He knew better.

"Something smells delicious."

He leaned in for a kiss, but she pressed two fingers to her lips. "Your mom might see us."

"We're not fifteen anymore. I think it's okay."

She leaned in and gave him a peck and then brushed by him.

"Talk about a drive-by," he said, the words dripping in disappointment.

She half shrugged. "There's always later. For now, taste that."

"What?"

"The coffee, silly." She entered the kitchen and held out a cup to his mom. "I brought you a special holiday blend I think will be the signature drink for the wedding."

"And yours—" she set the tray on the table, removed her cup, and lifted it as if to toast him "—Is a special blend carefully crafted just for you."

He lifted the paper cup to his lips but paused. "You're trying to whisper me, aren't you?"

She lifted a brow at him. "Just try it."

He sniffed the beverage, analyzing the aroma, and deduced that it had orange and cloves. Not good. He hadn't been able to even smell cloves since that one night in college. Should he tell her he didn't like cloves? Based on her expectant gaze, he wanted to like the drink or at least make her believe he did. He took a sip and forced a smile. "It's good."

She collapsed into the dining chair. "You hate it."

"No, I don't."

"You do. Your ear twitched."

He touched his ear. "No, it didn't."

His mom placed the plate of hot cakes on the table. "It did. Just like it always does when you lie."

"I have a tell?" He started to realize why he was so bad at poker.

"A glaring one. What don't you like about it?" Mary-Beth asked in a sad tone he would do anything to change.

He sighed and slid the cup toward her. "It has cloves in it or a spice like it. I don't like cloves."

"Since when?" she asked.

"Since I got food poisoning from a Taiwan restaurant in college. I can't even smell any type of five spice or cloves or I gag." He hated being the cause of her sadness. "Why is this so important to you?"

She held her own cup between her hands. "It just shows how little I know you."

"What? That's crazy."

His mom waved the spatula, her head, and anything else that could move at him like an airplane traffic controller.

Not sure what he'd done, but he understood the warning and went into repair mode. "I'm sorry. I didn't mean it that way."

The room fell you-stupid-man silent.

"Um, I'm so sorry, Mrs. McCadden. Serena called, and she can't open the store this morning. I just came by to bring you some coffee to say thanks for the invite." Mary-Beth made for the door.

"Wait." Tanner blocked her path, but his mom's spatula shooed him once more.

"Of course, dear. No worries. Let me just pack you some breakfast to go."

Mary-Beth turned away from him as if he were a stranger. "You don't need to do that."

"You'd be doing me a favor. I don't need these sitting around for me to eat." She grabbed a Tupperware container and slid some hot cakes, eggs, and bacon into it. Tanner only stood there dumbfounded, feeling like he had to do something, anything.

He grabbed the coffee and downed a gulp, certain he could pull off liking it, but he gagged. Not a little gag, but a run-to-the-sink, heaving kind of gag. The cloves were way too much for him to ignore.

"Here, hon. I'll walk you out." Only the sight of his mom's blue shirt moved in his peripheral vision.

He grabbed a dish towel, swiped the remanence from his lips, and then raced after her, but by the time he reached the door, his mom was like a fifty-foot-tall blockade against the enemy.

"You don't even think about going after her. We need to talk. Do you know nothing about women? I thought you were some sort of college stud. Maybe you are a clueless, self-absorbed one."

He winced, realizing part of her words were true, given his womanizing phase to overcompensate the loss of his football glory. It was short-lived and had left him empty inside. He wasn't that man now. "Ouch. Harsh much?"

"Only saying what I see, son." That darn spatula conducted him back to the kitchen. "Sit. We need to chat. You've heard of the birds and the bees, right?"

"Mother…"

She passed him his hot cakes. "Do you want me to fill you

in on what you did that was wrong? Because based on that dumb-as-mud expression you're wearing, you don't get it."

He grabbed his now-aching head. "Please."

"I'm going to share with you some Elder secrets that you need to never let them know I told you or I'll be erased from the Sugar Maple good-gossip line."

"Seriously? That's a real thing?"

"Promise or I'm out of here."

"Fine, promise." He looked at the once-mouthwatering cakes and didn't want to take a bite. His stomach still swished and swirled from that awful concoction.

"First off, you are dismissive of the fact that Mary-Beth is a Coffee Whisperer."

"She believes that? I mean really believes it?"

Mom gave him the shut-up-or-I'm-gone look, so he sealed his trap.

"Mary-Beth *is* the coffee whisperer. Believe it now, or you might as well walk, because that is her main identity. You have football. She has coffee."

"Okay, so I believe it."

"Nuh-uh. Don't even try to faux believe." She sat down and put that dreaded spatula on the table between them. "I need you to open your ears and hear me."

"I'm listening."

"No, you're not. You don't really believe in her shine. You don't like her coffee, so you think she's bad at her job. If you did believe, you'd understand that Mary-Beth has a 1000-0 undefeated record, and you are making it 1000-1. She's intuitive with people, knows them, understands them."

"But with me she can't get it right." He palmed his head. "And I just spewed all over her record."

"Exactly."

"But what was I supposed to do? I tried to drink it. You saw."

"Oh, I saw you fumble on a winning pass. What would you do if you were 0-1 at the state championship with ten seconds left on the clock? Nothing to lose but the game if you don't score on this last play. Would you run the same play that failed three downs in a row?"

"No."

"Then what do you think you should do?"

"Pull a Hail Mary," he said, but despite his words, his brain wasn't translating football to how to fix things with Mary-Beth. "But how do I do that? What's my next play? I mean, plan. Geesh, mom, stop with the football analogies and tell me what to do."

"You believe in her the way she's always believed in you. Make her the star of your relationship for once. Become the coffee groupie."

"Is that a thing?" He quirked a brow at her.

"It is now. Think about it. You chose a different school for the fame of playing for a team like Notre Dame. You chose that over your relationship."

"But I wanted her to come with me. It was going to be for us."

"No, Tanner. It was for you. She would've been an ornament on your Christmas tree of life. Don't you think it's her turn? Now, you go to that coffee shop, and you help her figure out what you like. Enjoy her tastings, be an active participant in her business. Suck it up and leave that football field long enough to show her you care about her life and her business and what she's good at."

"I *do* care. Of course I care. I'm proud of who she's become."

"Did you tell her that?"

He blinked at her. "No, but she knows."

His mom reached for that darn spatula again, and he shoved from the table. "If she doesn't, I'm going to tell her right now."

CHAPTER TWENTY-THREE

THE STRONG, successful, emotionally available, and solid Seth Dufour entered the shop and sat at the front counter. "Hey, there."

Mary-Beth straightened her apron and forced a friendly smile but wasn't in the mood to deal with guilt for not liking the perfect man on paper in front of her. Why did she have to care so much about a football-playing farmer who didn't understand business? "What can I get for you?"

"Anything that you'll make me. I trust you."

Why couldn't that be Tanner? "Actually, I was working on some samples for today. I've been wanting to try some new blends. Would you mind?"

He stood, removed his coat, set it on the back of the stool, and then sat down. "I'd be happy to, thanks. I enjoy being a part of creating new things. That's actually partly why I'm here. What you said the other night made me think about what I really wanted in life. Don't get me wrong, I'm not converting to being a farmer to win you over, but I will be changing my career. Yes, this is lucrative, but I'm into making things happen more than numbers. I'm going to start investing in some various businesses I believe in and helping them grow."

She mixed and steamed and poured. "That sounds exciting. I know I've found great joy in building this place." She looked around at the pictures on the walls that Jackie had ordered from some chic New York place that set the tone for the southern country couture look of her cafe. The countertops that Stella had installed, and the special serving dishes for parties resting on the back rack that Ms. Horton had given her. The dried floral arrangements from Felicia, and the glass cake container that Carissa gave her. This was her favorite place next to the lake and tree house.

"That's why I'm here. I'd love to hire you as a consultant to look over some coffee shops I'm considering backing. I want to know if you believe they are good investments."

She hesitated, not wanting to lead Seth on. Despite her confusion over her renewed attraction to Tanner, she was sure of one thing. Seth wasn't the right man for her. "I'm sorry, but I have to ask... Is this an excuse to spend time with me?"

He folded his hands as if in prayer and rested his elbows on the counter. "Yes, but not the only reason. I think you have the wrong impression of me, and I'd like an opportunity to show you I'm not a one-dimensional guy who only thinks of money."

"But..." She pushed several shot glasses in front of him. "Listen, my heart is still confused, and I'm all mixed up."

"I understand, and I promise I'm not desperate enough to push you into anything. You know, some women *want* to date me." He adjusted his tie, and there was no doubt the sophisticated, attractive man had women lining up for a chance to date him. She also knew a man like that liked a challenge, and that's what made him pursue her.

"I have no doubt."

"Listen, beyond my attraction to you, I can really use your help. Will you do it?" The sincerity of his words was etched in the lines around his wide eyes. She'd never seen him look that animated over his current job before.

She thought about it for a moment, but before she could answer, the front door opened and in strutted Tanner. "Sure, I'd be happy to," she said in a rush.

A few other people filtered in, and Tanner stood by like a lost puppy. Mary-Beth almost felt sorry for him as he watched Seth interact with her at the counter. Once the crowd cleared out, he shifted his stance, and she knew that look. He was readying for his big play.

"Hi there. I hope you don't mind, but I wanted to come in and try some of your coffee." He sounded less...sure of himself. The broad-shouldered, commanding man looked apprehensive.

"Okay, but give me a few minutes." She turned to Seth and leaned over the counter toward him. "So, what do you think of that one?"

"Delicious. Everything you make is delicious."

"Suck up much?" Tanner mumbled under his breath.

"And that one?" She pointed to the same drink she'd made for Tanner earlier.

Seth took another sip. "Ah, I think of a Christmas dinner next to a fire."

"Perfect. You get that flavor from the cloves."

Tanner gave a neanderthal grunt.

Seth put the cup down, eyed Tanner, and then eyed her. "I need to get to some meetings, but I'll come by later to see you. We can discuss what we talked about in more detail then."

She knew he was trying to lead Tanner to believe that their meeting later was a date, but she didn't correct him. "I look forward to it."

Seth made a quick exit, and Tanner slid into his chair as if he claimed the prime spot at Mary-Beth's counter. "Listen, I deserve that, but beyond football, I don't play games."

That sounded more like the commanding Tanner she knew. Why was it the traits that she found most sexy were also the most exasperating?

She didn't respond. She only placed four cups in front of him. He looked down at them as if she had set down poison. "Don't worry. None of them have any clove flavoring at all. Promise."

His shoulders relaxed, lowering from his ears, and he lifted one of the cups to his lips.

The store was unusually quiet around this time, with only Mrs. Sanchez in the corner knitting while sipping her tea. Mary-Beth held her breath and waited.

He lowered the cup and pressed his lips together. His tongue darted out and claimed the drop left behind. His face relaxed, and he smiled. "That's good."

A flicker of hope ignited inside her. "Here, try this one." He did and gave the same response, but it wasn't enough. "And this one?"

He obediently tried it and offered the same smile and nod. After he tasted the last one, she sighed.

He reached for her, capturing her wrist in his grasp. Heat surged up her arm, but it sizzled and expired. "What is it? I liked them all."

She offered a reassuring smile that it wasn't anything he

did wrong, but she pulled away from him. "I know. And I do appreciate you trying, but it's obvious I haven't found it."

"Found what?"

"That perfect blend for you. I don't understand why this is so difficult. I've never had to try this hard before."

"Maybe it's me, not you."

She picked up the spoon to stir up some more concoctions. "Oh no, you're not giving the 'it's me, not you' speech."

"I didn't mean it that way." His shoulders rose with his hands pressed to his lap. "What is it with women and kitchen utensils?" he mumbled half to himself.

"What?"

"Nothing. Listen." He walked around the counter, plied the spoon from her grasp, and then captured her hands in his. They stood front to front, shoulders to chest. "I want you to know how proud I am of you. Look at this place, this business you've created. I wish I could claim to have achieved so much with my life."

She didn't like it when he put himself down. "You have! You're a college football coach."

"Assistant coach, and to be honest, I haven't felt that adrenaline rush that I once did when I was on the field playing. It's a career, not a calling. This here... This is what you were meant to do. That is such a gift."

He touched her chin so she'd look into his piercing gray eyes that she swore could make her forget all her dreams in life. That frightened her more than anything else. She'd given up dance, and by the time she'd realized what she'd lost, it was too late. Too many years of not training and auditioning, and she'd known she had to find a new dream. And she had.

She ran her thumb over his farmer hands that were beginning to callus over already, as if they quickly remembered what working hard meant. "I'm sorry you don't feel that connection anymore."

"Oh, but I do. The minute I saw you when I returned here, the adrenaline rush was more intense than any winning touchdown I've ever made. You make me feel alive again. I don't need football, Mary-Beth. I only need you."

Her breath came in short bursts, and she could hold back no longer. She wrapped her arms around his neck and claimed his lips with all the intensity she'd been holding back since he'd arrived. What did it really mean that she couldn't make his perfect cup of coffee? He'd said such nice things to her, but he hadn't promised to stay. Not today. Not the other night. Not ever. But she was lost in him, and he returned her attention with an intensity that made her shiver inside. The feel of his arms around her, the firm claiming of her lips, the heartbeat pounding against her chest. Everything in the world washed away, and all that remained was their passion for each other.

CHAPTER TWENTY-FOUR

FARM WORK KEPT Tanner busy most of the day, but his mind and soul were consumed by that kiss. It sealed his desire to stay in Sugar Maple and work the farm. This would also give Hawk a chance to make a choice of staying in the military or coming home.

After Tanner finished his shower, he sat down at the kitchen table where his mom had left a snack of apples with peanut butter and he made some calls. In the farmhouse, all important decisions were made around the kitchen table— what college to attend, what team to play for, how to ask a girl on a date. So, it seemed like an appropriate place to work on Andy's future.

He dialed his recruiting buddy from UT and left a voice mail. "Hey, man. It's Tanner. I'm calling to tell you that I'm volunteering to help at a local high school in my hometown of Sugar Maple, and there's a kid here who is more talented than I have ever seen. Trust me when I tell you that you'll want to come see him play. If you're interested, the game's Friday night at seven. We'd be happy to host you out at our farmhouse while you're here. Thanks. I hope to see you then. Trust me, it won't be a wasted trip."

He made a few more calls at his old alma mater and a few other colleges where his name might mean something, and then all he could do was wait to see who showed. It was a long shot but possible. "Mama, I'm heading out to the field. I'll be home in a couple of hours," he called from the kitchen.

He decided it was rude to go outside without at least saying hello to the wedding crew. Besides, it gave him an excuse to catch a glimpse of Mary-Beth. He poked his head around the corner of the house to the garden. "Hello, ladies. How's the planning going?" His gaze traveled the circle of ladies, but he didn't spot Mary-Beth. Hopefully she wasn't with that Seth guy.

"If you're looking for your favorite barista, she bailed on us for a hot date at the coffeehouse with Seth," Jackie stated in her normal, I'm-ready-to-stir-up-trouble kind of way.

He swallowed a boulder-crushing curse before it left his lips. At that tidbit of information, he bolted from the garden and started his bike, ignoring his mom's words of warning in his head. These games needed to stop. He'd decided to stay, and it was time for her to believe him. He revved his bike and shot down the gravel drive, spitting pebbles behind him. His anger got the better of him, and he took the turn after the bridge too fast and skidded to a stop, narrowly avoiding a cow in the center of the road. He removed his helmet so he could breathe and took a second to let the stinging panic rush through him before he could move forward again.

By the time he reached Maple Grounds, his temper had thankfully cooled, but when he spotted Seth cuddled next to Mary-Beth at a bistro table, he parked his bike and rushed through the front door. "I need to speak to you."

She looked up at him, mouth open.

"Now," he ordered in a tone reminiscent of his father. He cringed at the notion.

"I'm so sorry. Would you excuse me for a moment?" She offered Seth a reassuring smile and Tanner a glower.

He waited in her office, heat radiating from his scalp. When she turned the corner, he opened his mouth to tell her she was being unfair and she needed to make a decision if he was the right man for her.

"What's going on?" she asked in an innocent tone.

"What's going on? Why are you still dating him? Have I not done enough to prove to you that I am here because of you? I'm working with the kids at the high school, calling college football scouts, tasting coffee, and tiptoeing around trying not to make you mad. What do you want from me?"

Her lips pressed together, and she crossed her arms over her chest with that set jaw that told him he'd crossed a line and run another mile past it. "First of all, I didn't ask you to be here for me. Secondly, I asked on behalf of Andy for you to help some kids out coaching the game, something I thought you'd enjoy. I didn't do it to keep you here or trap you to stay with me."

"That's not what I meant."

"Isn't it? You went to fulfill your dreams, and you haven't yet. And until you do, you're never going to stay here. I wouldn't want you to stay here for me. Stay or go. I don't care anymore. It's your decision. I won't hold it against you. At least this time you didn't promise to always be with me."

"That's not fair. We were kids. Manipulated, confused children who knew nothing about life."

"That doesn't give you a reason to come in here and order me to end my meeting early with Seth."

He stumbled back, realization washing over him. "Meeting?"

"Yes, meeting. It's not a date. I'm helping him look over some coffeehouses he's thinking about investing in as a new business opportunity for him. And, for your information, I told Seth the other night that I couldn't date him because I was confused about how I felt about you and our future. But you didn't trust me. You assumed I was playing games. Or are you just looking for an excuse to prove to yourself you made the right decision all those years ago? Just because football didn't work out doesn't mean that I'm your fallback plan."

"No, that's not true." Tanner closed the distance between them, desperate to make this right. "You don't mean that."

"I do. And you can stop bullying me. I'm not your mother."

"Bully?" The word kicked him in the gut, and he thought he'd be doubled over for life.

The anger faded from her face, and she reached for him. "Tanner."

"No." He left in a huff, needing to collect his thoughts before he said anything else he'd regret. The last thing he ever wanted to be was like his father.

CHAPTER TWENTY-FIVE

"WHAT DID TANNER DO, and should I go beat him up?" Stella nudged Knox out of the way to let Mary-Beth know they didn't have to do the meeting if there was too much drama going on in her life.

"No. It isn't only about him. It's something I said." Mary-Beth settled in for an uncomfortable meeting about her Coffee Whisperer abilities—or lack thereof.

"I doubt it. You could never say anything mean to anyone. That's my job." Stella allowed Knox to sit down but held her hand over his laptop so he wouldn't open it.

"I called him a bully. I compared him to his father." Shame filled Mary-Beth.

"Ouch." Stella couldn't even hide her wince, but she recovered quickly. "Well, I'm sure he deserved it. What did he do?"

Mary-Beth dropped her head into her hands, unable to face the reality of her epic fail. "He came to declare his affection for me because he thought I was dating Seth."

"What? I can't hear you. Sit up." Stella tried to be supportive, and Mary-Beth knew she was in her own way. The girl would do anything to protect a friend, but she'd also tell you how it was, even if you didn't want to know. She was the tough-love type.

Mary-Beth faced Stella, Knox, and her mistake. "I said he came to declare his love for me and to promise that I meant more to him than football."

The front door chimed, but Stella shot up and ushered poor Mr. Laden, who worked at the recreation department, out the door.

"You do know I need customers to run a business…"

"Give him free coffee next time. That always works on me," Stella returned, and this time Knox put his arm around her.

"What my sweet bride-to-be is trying to ask is why did you get upset when he told you he cared so much for you?"

"That's what I asked," Stella grumbled, but leaned into Knox, the Stella Whisperer. Only he could calm her like no other.

Mary-Beth thought back to when Tanner had decided to take the scholarship to Notre Dame. She'd never felt so betrayed before, and the loss had been so great, she thought it would swallow her up and spit her out. She'd chosen to not pursue dance once his football schedule became so intense. If she had, they never would've gotten to see each other because he was always at practice or a game and she was always at rehearsals or recitals or working at the studio to earn class time. It had been her choice, and she'd never regretted it until that day Tanner made that big announcement. He'd chosen football over their plans. "It's hard to explain, but I know deep down that I'm a consolation prize for a life he wanted but didn't get. I guarantee that if he got a call tomorrow to go play ball for a pro team, he'd be gone."

"But that can't happen, right?" Knox took advantage of Stella's distraction and opened his laptop. "I mean, his injury took him out."

"Yes, but that doesn't matter. What happens if something else comes along and he leaves again?" A heat deep in her belly rose to her chest. "It's difficult to explain, but I have this feeling that he's not going to stay."

"Do you think that's why you can't make him a special coffee?" Knox's fingers touched the keys, but when Stella shot him a sideways glare, he retreated from his laptop.

"Maybe. I don't know. I think I'm getting closer. We did a tasting this morning, and he liked what I made." A dash of hope sprinkled over her doubt.

"That's good, right?" Knox asked.

"I guess. Maybe if I had more time, but he keeps wanting too much too fast." She wrung her hands, a nervous energy making her long to move far from this conversation.

Knox closed his laptop and stood. "I have an idea."

A zap of warning jolted Mary-Beth. "Listen, I know you want me to be this perfect Coffee Whisperer, but I can't be. It won't work for the show, not when I have failed over and over with Tanner. I'm too confused. I mean, our relationship didn't make it before, no matter how much we loved each other. How can we work through things now?"

Stella leaned across the table, shocking Mary-Beth with her gentle touch. "Because you two belong together. You always have, and you always will. And great love is worth the wait. Trust me."

Were those tears in Stella's eyes? Before Mary-Beth could say another word, Stella retreated, using her faux leather jacket to swipe her tears, and she ushered Knox to the front door, ending their meeting before it had ever started. How that man had chiseled through the rock-hard exterior of Stella Frasier, Mary-Beth would never know.

Knox held the door open for Stella and looked back at Mary-Beth. "Get to work and have some samples ready. We'll be back in an hour when you close for a private tasting."

Mary-Beth wasn't sure she liked where this was going. If it weren't for Stella, she would walk away from the Knox Brevard show. She couldn't disappoint Stella's fiancé, and not to mention that if she didn't do the show, would that affect Jackie's segment? No, Mary-Beth had made a commitment, and unlike other people, she would never break her word.

Mary-Beth went to work, mixing, concocting, and tasting different blends between serving customers and decided on six of the best.

The sun dipped below the mountain, leaving streaks of auburn and gold with twinkling stars. A beautiful fall night so inviting she stepped outside and closed her eyes to breathe in the scents of autumn. There was no place in the world like Sugar Maple this time of year. She'd always belonged here and always knew she wanted to stay. Her phone buzzed in her pocket, interrupting her moment, and she saw it was her mother, finally returning her call.

After a deep breath, she answered. "Hello."

"Hi, how are you and Andy doing?" Her mother sounded tired, not surprising since she'd always been overworked.

"We're good. How are you and Dad?" Mary-Beth wanted to skip the pleasantries, but she knew it was important not to put her mother on the defensive if she was going to get anywhere with their conversation.

"We're good. Are you calm enough to talk now?"

Mary-Beth abandoned her moment of fall bliss and

returned to the inside of the coffee shop for a private conversation. "I'm working on it, but I'm calm enough to talk."

"Okay, so I ask for you to listen before you start yelling at me."

"I didn't yell, but yes, I promise to listen." Mary-Beth paced the coffee shop, looking at everything, as if she needed a distraction to control her temper.

"Okay, here I go." A breath blew into the phone with a whistle before her mother began. "Your father and I saw how you struggled with your relationship with Tanner. He was a god in our town, but you were never one to follow or be left behind. At the games, you were abandoned on the sidelines, watching. You stopped pursuing your love of dance and attended more practices and games. When Tanner announced he'd go to UT on a football scholarship, you had forgotten about your childhood dream of going to New York to try out for a dance scholarship. It was as if you had no direction in your life except Tanner."

Mary-Beth hated the fact that she saw the truth in her mother's words. She wanted to argue, but being forced to listen without interrupting meant she actually had to remember the words long enough for a rebuttal. That allowed the truth to sink in.

Her mother continued without pausing. "What we did wasn't right, but it's what we thought was best. We wanted to protect you, and when Tanner decided to run off to Notre Dame, he expected you to drop everything. You'd already decided to try out for the dance team, and you were excited to be close enough to home to visit on weekends whenever you wanted because you knew you'd miss Andy. I didn't want Tanner deciding your entire future for you before you were old enough and experienced enough to decide it for yourself."

Mary-Beth slipped and said, "It should've been my decision," but her mother ignored the comment and continued.

"I doubted our decision, and we were going to tell you both at Christmas, but after Tanner was injured and couldn't play ball, there was no way I was going to tell you the truth."

"Why not? Then he could've moved back to UT to be with me."

"Because love at seventeen isn't like love at thirty, forty, or fifty. When you're young, anything is possible, but when the reality of an ex-career turned mediocre living becomes your future, you grow resentful. I wanted you to be more than that. I wanted you to be independent and not have to worry about the man making the money because you gave up everything to follow his dreams and you find yourself home raising children you can't afford, working two shifts a day, tired, and broken by the time you're forty, hoping to give your kids a future, only to see them throwing it away." Her mother's voice broke, and sobs sounded muffled from the other side of the phone.

Her mother never cried. Not when their first house was foreclosed on after Dad lost some money in a bad investment, or when the car was repossessed when no one needed private lessons on the piano, or when they ate pasta for a month because Dad lost his job at the factory. "Mom, are you okay?"

"Yes, I am, but I need you to understand why."

"I think I do." Her father had been the fun, free-spirited one who never got in Mary-Beth's way and made her believe anything was possible, while her mother grounded her when she wanted to fly away. "But it still didn't give you the right to lie to me, to break us up and keep us apart for so long."

"It's not too late. Go to him now and tell him how you feel, and you can be together. You can hate me for the rest of your life, but I'm proud of the successful woman you've become. You're everything I ever wanted you to be, and now I know you can financially handle your future and any whim Tanner decides to drag you on. Go to him now."

Mary-Beth didn't know what to say. She wanted to run into Tanner's arms more than anything, but something still held her back. Fear. The fear of losing him all over again. The fear he'd never be happy without more in his life. The fear that her mother was right. "Can I ask you something, Mom?"

"Yes, anything."

"Do you still love Dad? I mean, after all he's put you through, would you change the fact you married him?"

Mary-Beth expected her to take a minute or avoid the question, but she answered without thought. "No, because I have you and Andy. I wouldn't trade you two for anything, not even all the riches in the world and an easy life. That's the only reason I feel guilty over what I did to you. But I still believe if you were meant to be together, you can be together now and have an easier life. And that would have made all of this worth it. That is, if you still want to be with him."

Her mother's words hung in the air like a gnat she couldn't swat away. "I love Tanner in a way I have never and will never love anyone else. But, honestly, I don't know."

"Why?" her mother said in a surprisingly steady tone.

"I think it's because if he left me once, despite the circumstances, what will stop him from leaving me again, or worse, what if he wants to take me away from everything the way Dad always took you away? How do I know that I won't resent him later if he does? Do you resent Dad?"

Her mother didn't say anything for several seconds. "Sometimes. Marriage is complicated and can be difficult, but at the end of the day, when I crawl into bed, the only arms I want to hold me are your father's."

In that moment, Mary-Beth knew she needed to take a chance, because there was no man in the world she'd want to ever be held by but Tanner McCadden.

CHAPTER TWENTY-SIX

"TRUST ME, THIS IS A GOOD IDEA." Knox Brevard, a man on a mission, blocked Tanner's path to his motorcycle.

The body odor of a few nearby players reminded Tanner he wasn't alone, so he squared his shoulders. "No, it's not. Things are complicated right now between Mary-Beth and me. I don't think sticking a camera in our faces will help things. I'm not into reality television."

"It's not like that," Stella said, inserting herself into the conversation. "Listen, you know me. You know I would only ask you to do this if I thought it would help Mary-Beth. I would never cause her any more pain, and if I thought your football mentality would get in the way, I'd race you out of town myself on our bikes."

He looked to Andy, who eavesdropped while acting as if he was collecting equipment to return to the locker room. "What do you think, kid?"

Andy dropped the bag of helmets and waved for a teammate to take care of the rest of the job. "You should do it. Knox's show has saved this town from financial ruin. It'd help

Mary-Beth's business if she was on his show. Besides, I'm hoping you're gonna stick around, because otherwise I can't leave Mary-Beth here alone. She has a ton of friends, but friends aren't family."

"I just called several recruiters and put my name out there on your behalf, and now you tell me this?"

"I'm a teenager. I'm not supposed to be reliable." He shrugged and strutted off, leaving Tanner with Stella and Knox and their proposal to deal with.

A whistle blew in the distance, probably another sports team ending practice with the setting sun. "And you sure she wants me to come back to Maple Grounds? She made it clear she didn't want me bullying her into anything."

"Men!" Stella stomped off, leaving Knox behind.

Knox chuckled. "Trust me, you're never going to understand them. You just have to love them. Do you want Mary-Beth in your life or not?"

Tanner didn't even have to think about his answer. "Yes, more than anything I've wanted in a long time."

Knox clapped his shoulder. "Then what do you have to lose?"

Tanner found his words ominous. The last person who said that to him was his father, when he nudged him to go see Notre Dame. "Fine."

The short distance to the town square was enough to make him nervous. Mary-Beth had him running circles with no mapped-out plays. He hated not knowing what to do. Had it been this complicated when they were teens?

When he walked inside, he prepared himself for another onslaught of angry words and accusations, but Mary-Beth tentatively walked over and stood a breath from him.

"I want to apologize."

He looked down at her, trying to read her, but couldn't. "I don't understand."

She crooked a finger around one of his. "I never should've called you a bully. You're nothing like your father. I was scared."

His tense muscles softened, and he closed the space between them, ignoring the bell at the door announcing Knox and Stella's arrival. "Of what? Me? I'm sorry I came barging in here like that. Jealousy can make a man stupid."

"Then it can make a girl an idiot." She bit her bottom lip, and he allowed her time to collect her thoughts before asking any more questions or bulldozing through everything. "I was jealous all those years of football. Most women worshiped you for the game, but I started to resent giving up everything for you. I didn't understand what I was so scared of until I spoke to my mother."

He studied her expression, expecting hostility but finding softness instead. "You spoke to her?"

"Yes, and she made me see how much I gave up the first time we were together."

He grabbed her hand tight. "I never wanted you to give up anything for me. I wanted to play ball so I could afford to give you the world, but now I'm only a poor farmer."

"I never cared about fame and fortune." Her thumb brushed distractingly over his knuckles.

He wanted to show her that she was everything and football meant nothing without her. The longing to see her again had plagued him for years. "Then what did you care about?"

"You. That was the problem. It wasn't your fault, but I gave up everything I was interested in to be with you. I gave up dancing so I could meet you after practice and we could sneak off to our hideout for a couple of hours. I gave up hanging out with my friends on Friday nights after the games because I wanted to be with you. I gave up auditioning to go to New York so we could go to UT."

"I never knew. You told me that you lost interest in dance and only did it to keep your mother happy."

"I told you that so you wouldn't convince me to continue because it would mean less time for us."

Mary-Beth's hands trembled, and he took them both, kissing each of them and holding them to his chest. "I'm sorry I didn't see it. I was young and selfish and wanted football and you. I should've thought about what you wanted."

"I never felt like I gave anything up because I always had you and that's what I wanted." Her eyes misted, and he knew she was struggling not to cry, but that's when he saw it, what he'd done when he'd accepted the scholarship to Notre Dame. He'd broken her trust in their future and in their love.

"Until you didn't have me." He swallowed through the rise of regrets. They stood there looking at each other, as if seeing the real person behind the emotions. "I understand now why you're afraid, and I'll stop pushing so hard. You'll see how much I care and how you can have what you want this time around. I'll be helping at football practice and working the farm and spending every spare moment I have proving my loyalty to you." He released her hand and put his palm to her chest, covering the ring hanging from the chain around her neck. "And someday, when you're ready, you'll trust me with your heart again."

She sniffled and closed her eyes. "Thank you."

He leaned down, wanting to kiss her, to love her, to be with her always, but he restrained himself and only said. "You'll see. Nothing will pull me away from you. Not now, not in the future, not ever."

CHAPTER TWENTY-SEVEN

FOR TWO DAYS, Mary-Beth worked on various flavorful concoctions before the big *Coffee Whisperer winning her man back* coffee tasting. For some reason, she hadn't anticipated that they were actually going to film it. In her mind, it was only going to be a tasting, not an internet-worthy segment. Apparently, that was also what Tanner had thought, since he hadn't even showered after practice.

"Ignore the camera and focus on the coffee and Tanner," Knox said in his director tone at her.

Mary-Beth hadn't expected a full film crew, not to mention Drew, Knox, and their assistant Lori all huddled around them, directing and fetching and changing lighting. "I'm trying, but you're distracting me."

Tanner reached over the counter and touched her arm, and she swore she could feel the lens constricting to get a close up of his touch. "Look at me. Together we can do this. Unless you don't want to, then I'm out of here." He tilted his head, allowing his sexy post-practice hair to fall over like an exclamation point to his stunning eyes.

"No, let's just get this over with." She stood straight and shook her hands out. "Try this one." She tapped the rim of the cup and held her breath until he took a drink and smiled.

"I like this one. It's really good."

"Progress," she mumbled under her breath.

Knox did a lifting motion and pointed to his mouth.

"What? I said it's great." Tanner sat back in his seat and wiped his palms down his pants like he did when he was figuring something out. "But it isn't *the* drink."

She nodded and took the cup away.

"Wait, can you tell me what's in it?"

No way she was going to give any secrets away, so she leaned over and whispered in her ear. "Tell me what you tasted that you liked."

His eyes traveled to her lips the way they did right before he kissed her. He brushed his cheek to hers, placed his lips against her ear, and whispered, "There was a heaviness to it but with a sweet undertone."

Warm breath caressed her ear, causing goose bumps to flare up, covering her skin. He caught sight of her breathy reaction and tweaked her nose. "Later, when the cameras are turned off."

Stella cleared her throat. "Um, still running over there."

"Thanks for the reminder." Mary-Beth took cup number two and passed it to him. "And this one?"

He took a hesitant sip, as if worried this wasn't the one either. And it wasn't. She didn't even have to ask. The man's ears moved before he even opened his mouth to lie.

"Next," she said loud enough for the internet to hear.

After the last two, she tried to not show her frustration, but she looked to Knox and said, "Sorry. I told you this was a bad idea."

"No, it's great. Perfect."

"But you're doing a show on the Coffee Whisperer, and I can't...well, whisper my boyfriend."

"Boyfriend?" Tanner sat up straight. "Oh, well, I don't know about that. I mean, it's awful sudden."

She grabbed the dish rag and snapped it at him. He jumped out of the way, grabbed it, and rushed around the counter after her.

"That's a wrap for now. One more thing." Knox called after them as they raced around the kitchen like small children.

"What's that?" Mary-Beth made it to Stella, halting Tanner's advance.

Lori held out a document. "We want to do a feature about your brother with the coaches coming to see him play on Friday. Do we have your permission to interview him? He'll be able to use the footage for social media and to show scouts who can't make it to see him play."

Mary-Beth studied the document and knew she'd have to get someone who understood these kinds of contracts better to read over it, but more importantly, she wanted to know one thing. "I need to ask Andy about it and get back to you."

"By tomorrow morning, so we have time to set up for the big game tomorrow night?" Lori insisted.

Mary-Beth eyed the back door where Andy usually came in after practice. "Sure. I think I can get back to you by then."

Lori smiled. "Great. It'll be good for Andy."

Mary-Beth mindlessly toyed with the ring hanging from the chain. If all of this went well, she planned to tell Tanner after the game that she was tired of being scared and she was ready to move forward to see where things went between them. Once everyone cleared out, she found him sniffing and tasting various things in her kitchen. "What are you doing?"

"Trying to figure out what I like. If we do, then you'll trust that we're meant to be together."

She walked up behind him and slid her arms around his waist, pressing her cheek to his back. "I never thanked you."

"For what?"

"For helping coach Andy's team when you said you were done with football and for calling the scouts to see him play." She squeezed tighter. "Does it bother you to be back on your old high school practice field? I'm worried about how this will make you feel on game night. I know I'm a little late. I should've thought about that before dragging you into all this."

"I'm good. Don't worry about me." He turned in her arms and raked his fingers through her hair with mesmerizing comfort. "I might not be playing the game, but I'm finding it enjoyable to work with high school players more than college. It's less commercial, and I have more freedom with what I'm doing with the players."

The way his eyes lit up under the dim lights of the coffee shop told her it really did provide joy for him. "I'm glad."

The back door swung open, and Andy raced in on cleated feet.

"What are you doing? You know better than to wear those things in here. You'll damage the hardwood."

"Sorry." He bent over and yanked them off his feet, sending dirt and grass everywhere. "Is it true? The principal told me that I'm going to be interviewed on Knox Brevard's show and that the scout from University of Tennessee is making a trip all the way down here to see me play."

"Yes, it's true," Mary-Beth said, elated at the sight of Andy's happiness.

He grabbed his cleats and ran around like a jack rabbit on

two espressos. "Come on, coach. I need you to help. I've got to practice."

"I think we've practiced enough for today," Tanner said, holding tight to Mary-Beth, as if he didn't want to let her go for anything else in the world. Not even football.

"It's fine." Mary-Beth reluctantly moved from his arms. "I know you'd rather be outside playing football than in here helping me close up shop."

He pulled her back into him. "No, I'm where I want to be."

"Don't worry. After the game tomorrow, we'll have all weekend together."

"Our entire lives together, you mean." He kissed her cheek and left her standing in her kitchen believing happy endings were really possible.

CHAPTER TWENTY-EIGHT

THE HIGH SCHOOL band rumbled through the evening with pounding drums and tooting tubas, taking Tanner back to his youth. Intoxicating excitement wafted in the air, along with the smell of popcorn and hotdogs from the concession stands. All of Sugar Maple had come to see the star football player, Andy Richards, lead them to victory against their Creekside rivals. In that moment, Tanner flashed back to a decade ago before he ran out to a crowd cheering his name.

Trumpets announced a welcome for the team to enter the field. Nervous energy jolted him into gear, rushing the players through the paper gates held by the cheerleaders. The fans erupted in applause.

Adrenaline pumped through him like he'd be playing for his town again. How he'd missed those cheers. He wasn't a vain person, but he loved to make the town proud.

Creekside made their entrance with cheers from the opposing side. He swore he saw that loudmouth Cathy Mitchell who used to boo him in his youth each time he scored. Tanner fought his nerves and scanned the stands until he found Mary-Beth settled in the center of the Fabulous Five. He couldn't help but feel that their support meant the team would come out victorious.

"Tanner McCadden." His scout buddy from UT approached, his balding head reflecting the stadium lights. "I was excited to receive your call."

"Jackson, thanks so much for making the trip. You won't regret it. Andy Richards is the most gifted player I've ever seen."

"That's a high praise coming from you. I'm still bitter that you were stolen by Notre Dame." The man had a big, friendly, toothy smile. "I don't plan on letting that happen again." He shook Tanner's hand. "How's the knee these days anyway?"

"Good. It tells me when we'll have a thunderstorm, and I set off metal detectors at the airport, so it's functional for everyday use."

The team rushed to the sidelines, and the refs took the field.

"Excuse me, I need to get with my players. Please, make yourself at home. You can stay here or relax in the stands. After the game, you can follow me back to the farm."

"Thanks for the offer, but I can't stay. We'll chat before I leave, though. If you don't mind, I'll hang here with you."

Tanner offered a nod of approval and went to talk to the team before the game started. "You boys are ready for this."

"Is that the scout?" Andy asked, standing on his toes and peering around Tanner.

He snagged Andy's face mask and turned him to keep his attention on the game. "You ignore that man over there and focus. This isn't the Andy Richards show. This is about your team, not you. Got me?"

"Gotcha, Coach."

The scoreboard rolled backwards from 99 until it hit zero. The band played a war song, and the cheerleaders chanted for victory. Tanner finished his coaching duties and sent Andy out for the coin toss with the other captain.

They won and chose to receive. He'd worked so hard with the team and developed plays that harnessed the strengths of each individual player. With Andy as their wide receiver, all the quarterback had to do was get the ball into his hands.

Tanner clapped and found himself jumping up and down with the players to keep his muscles warm out of habit. He needed to show professionalism to the town behind him, so he forced himself to appear a calm he didn't feel. He cared more about this game than he had about any of the college games he'd worked on for the last several years. Maybe it was because he had the freedom to organize the entire team, the plays, and be in charge of it all.

With the teams set at the line of scrimmage, Tanner said a silent prayer and the ball snapped. The Sugar Maple quarterback threw a perfect spiral. Andy went long, jumped like a kangaroo on a trampoline, and caught the ball like it was glued to his chest.

The crowd roared.

He landed.

And fumbled.

"Booo!" The crowd turned on Andy before he could retrieve the ball and toss it to the nearby ref. The infamous Cathy Mitchell from Creekside cheered and heckled Andy.

"Shake it off. You're just warming up!" Tanner shouted at him.

Andy bounced and flung his hands to stay loose. They positioned for the second play. Their quarterback did a fake and then passed it to Andy, who ran right into a lineman and went down. The ball slipped out from under him and tumbled across the field.

Tanner flashed back to his big day. The anxiety, the pressure to impress the scouts so intense he thought he'd collapse from blood pumping so fast through his ears.

Third play.

Set up.

Snap.

Run.

The ball sailed over the opposing team and right over Andy's head.

Tanner knew as coach the team deserved better. It would destroy Andy to pull him from the game—and possibly cause Mary-Beth another reason to get mad at him—but he had a duty to the other players and to the town. He signaled the exchange, and Andy rushed to him. By the time he reached Tanner, he was breathless and looked like he'd been charged by a herd of three-hundred-pound linebackers.

"Coach, don't pull me. I swear I got this. I've got to impress the scouts. You of all people should understand."

"I understand that the scouts mean nothing to your team. Ultimately, you are one person. Do you want to let down the boys out there who have been supporting you all season or the town who came out to see you play again? They have backed you as the star. It's your turn to back them. That team is ruling our game. Is that what you want? To be their punching bag?"

"No, Coach."

"I want you to forget about your chance at college fame and give your best to your high school team. The team that got you this far. You got me?"

"Yes, Coach." Andy's face morphed from wide-eyed terrified to angry-brow charge.

"Then when this play ends, you get yourself out there and you do it for the team."

"Yes, Coach."

Sugar Maple managed to advance enough to make a first down, but then only nudged it another five yards on the next three downs. Tanner believed in his team and took a chance. Calling an Abraham. He knew Andy needed one good play, a Hail Mary, and he'd be back in the game. He knew that if he didn't, UT and every other college team would write him off and never return. It was all or nothing with this play.

He knew that the team—and fans—probably thought he was crazy to run another play instead of punting this early in the game, but sometimes a coach had to go with his gut.

With eyes closed, he took a breath and listened as the quarterback hollered the cadence, but he opened them wide to watch the ball snap. Andy dodged a lineman, vaulted over two downed players, and ran like he was possessed by a greyhound.

The stands fell silent.

Opposing players went for the quarterback. He released the ball, and it glided high and far, straight for Andy, who waited at the ten-yard line.

Linemen pursued, ready to tackle, but Andy didn't budge. Instead, he stood his ground fearlessly and jumped with arms outstretched, tipping the ball with his fingers. He brought it down and caught it in a cradle. The crowd cheered as Andy raced to the end zone. The spectators erupted with excitement. And in that moment, Tanner knew Andy could do anything on the field, as long as he didn't let politics fog his brain.

The game played out until Sugar Maple dominated 28-7 and the final whistle blew. Tanner found himself breathless with excitement for his team. *That* was football. *That* was the game he loved.

When the celebration settled and the people dispersed, Jackson slapped Tanner on the back. "Good game. I'm glad I made the trip."

Tanner couldn't help but feel the pride of a job well done. "I told you Andy was the real deal."

"I have a confession to make. I'm not only here to report back about Andy. The offensive lineman coach is going to transfer, so there'll be an opening. You interested?"

"Head coach for the offensive line?" Mary-Beth's voice broke through the pounding in his ears at the invitation and shattered his excitement with one devastated glance from the woman he loved and the anguish in her gaze.

CHAPTER TWENTY-NINE

MARY-BETH DIDN'T GO HOME, knowing Andy was out cele-brating with his friends at the diner. Instead, she went to the tree house and sat inside, holding the gold ring Andy had bought for her in her hand. Somehow, she'd known this would happen. The minute she started to believe in the possi-bility of their future together, he'd leave.

She didn't cry. She only sat cross-legged on the ground, feeling more alone than she had in her entire life. Stella had urged her to join the celebration at the diner, but knowing that Tanner would be there had only driven her away. She needed time to be alone to face the truth.

It would always be his life over hers, and she wasn't sure she could do that, not after watching her mother follow her father's will for so long. But she couldn't ask him to stay either. It was ironic that she faced the same choice now that her parents had made for her all those years ago. For the first time, she was thankful for the time to grow and mature before making such a major decision.

Could she even think about selling her coffeehouse she'd

worked so hard to grow into a thriving business so she could move to Knoxville? If Andy moved there, it wouldn't be so bad, but he'd be busy with football and school. Tanner would be busy coaching, and what would she do? Would she be a supportive wife living in the cold, hard stands for the next twenty years?

She unhooked the chain and slid the ring off. It was adorable and beautiful and perfect. She knew he must've used the money he'd saved for college to buy it. There was no doubt in her mind that Tanner loved her. She knew that now. It wasn't about if he chose her over the game. It was that she didn't want him to.

And she would never make him decide. This time, she'd make the choice for him. She placed the ring inside the tin box and returned it to the hidden compartment. It was time to let go of the dream that would never be and move on with her life. And football was not her life.

She climbed down and walked through the dark woods, holding her lantern and allowing the tears to flow. It was time to mourn so she could heal. When she parked behind the coffee shop, she could hear the cheers from the diner and smiled, happy for her brother and for Tanner.

"Why did you leave without talking to me?" Tanner called down from her apartment steps above the shop.

She froze. She'd known she'd have to face him eventually but had thought she'd at least have until morning. "I thought you'd be celebrating with the team."

"Not without you. None of it is worth anything without you."

He took the steps two at a time and landed at the curb by her side. "I never asked for him to come here and offer the coaching job to me. I won't take it."

"Yes, you will. I'll never keep you from your dreams." She forced her voice not to waver, despite her fading desire to remain strong.

He grabbed her arms and squeezed, as if to make her focus on him and him only. "I love you," he said.

"I love you, too. That's why you need to go. Please, speak with them and check out the job offer. If it isn't our time to be together, that's okay."

"If not now, when?" He released her, stepping back and clutching his head as if a sudden migraine would strike him down. "Don't do this. Give us a chance."

"I am, by letting you go." She rose onto her toes and kissed the corner of his mouth. "Call me. I'll need your advice with Andy's future."

"I'll do better than that. We'll take him to colleges together to see what's out there," Tanner yelled after her, but she rushed up the stairs, into her apartment, and shut her door before she changed her mind.

When Andy returned home, she refused to give him any clue about her heart being broken because of football, not when he was on a high. "Why didn't you join us to celebrate?"

"I didn't want to crowd you. It was your moment, your time to be with your friends and enjoy your victory. I was so proud of you tonight, though." Mary-Beth forced the brightest smile she didn't feel.

"What's wrong?" Andy asked. "Did Coach Tanner break your heart again? I don't care what kind of opportunity he dangles in front of me. He can't treat my sister that way."

"Stop." Mary-Beth couldn't help but laugh. A stress-relieving, wild kind of laugh.

"What's so funny?"

The teenage boy she'd been charged to care for had been her everything the last couple of years.

"Nothing. It's just that you've grown up into a handsome, charismatic, amazing young man who I'm lucky to have as a brother."

Andy huffed and plopped down on the sofa. "You mean the kid you've been stuck with since our parents took off?"

"Don't be so hard on them. They're just trying to live life the best they can. That's all any of us can do."

"Wow, who are you? Since when do you defend the 'rents?" Andy apparently already forgot about charging out to defend her honor. He yawned. Obviously, the football high was fading.

She sat by his side and tossed the afghan over him. "You know having you here hasn't been a burden at all. It's been a joy in my life. I hope you'll come home from college whenever you can visit. I'm so glad we had these years together. I'm so proud of you."

They snuggled up on the couch, and Andy was asleep before he could mumble something about being a college football star. His words drove her from the living room, and she went down to her shop.

Unnerving quiet filled the empty shop, except for the drip that she needed to fix at the sink. She'd been happy here running her coffee shop, and she could be happy here again.

The night lasted an eternity, with the orange globe of the harvest moon shining through the front windows. The moon she once thought she'd see from the front porch of the farmhouse while watching her children run around chasing fireflies.

In the morning, Andy came down before school and joined her for breakfast. "You know, I'll be graduating at the end of this year, and I have friends I can live with until then. You don't have to stay. I can take care of myself now."

She jolted out of her wayward sadness and looked at him. "No. Not happening, so get that out of your head. I want to keep you as long as I can. I'll be the big sis you have to beg to stop sending you food and visiting campus for every event. You can't get rid of me. I'm like good old-fashioned Sugar Maple syrup that sticks to you until you wash me away."

He laughed, which made her laugh, but the joy was fleeting.

"Do you really think they're going to offer him the job? I mean, he'd be one of the youngest offensive coordinators in the history of college ball."

The pride in his voice hadn't escaped her. "He's that good. And he deserves it. I'm happy for him."

Andy downed the last of his milk and cleared his plate. "You know, Knoxville isn't that far. It isn't like he's returning to Indiana."

"I know, but it isn't about that." Mary-Beth took a sip of her coffee, savoring the feel-good pumpkin, cream, and cinnamon. "He needs to be free to focus on his life, not be trapped in a small town. When we were kids, all he wanted to do was break free of this place. We had plans to take on the world, but to be honest, once I was apart from him, I realized I didn't want all that. I wanted home and family and community. We weren't meant to be together. We're too different. It's time for me to be me and him to be him."

"Even if it makes you both miserable?" Andy asked with the innocence of youth.

She had no answer, so she pulled her best motherly card. "You better go before you're late for school."

All day, she mindlessly served clients, but her heart wasn't in it. Several orders were mixed up, and she burned her hand on the milk frothier. *Ugh.* She needed to get a grip. Tanner McCadden was never going to turn down the opportunity of his career to be home with her and a teenage boy, a farm, and small-town community. Not when he'd tasted the sweet flavors of success.

CHAPTER THIRTY

FOR SEVERAL DAYS, Tanner tried to convince Mary-Beth that they could work through this, but she wouldn't listen. The only thing left to do was to go speak with the powers that be at UT.

The drive through the beautiful mountains with his windows down made Tanner feel free and alive. It reminded him of his first day returning to Tennessee. The charm of the south without the small-town suffocation. Not that he had hated growing up in Sugar Maple. There were just not any opportunities except working yourself to death on the farm like his father had.

Tanner pulled over at an overlook and reached for his phone to share a picture with Mary-Beth but stopped himself. She'd made it plain that he needed to go after his dreams and that she wouldn't speak to him again unless he did. Of course, she was right. He'd worked so hard to move up in the industry. Always the first one in and the last one out the door every day. All the other coaches had families and responsibilities, but his life was football. It had been for as long as he could remember.

The drive continued to weave around the peaks, and mist floated in with a damp, lonely feel to it. He shut the windows and concentrated on the road ahead. This was his big break. He wanted to share it with someone, but his mom couldn't leave the farm for the day, and he'd assumed Mary-Beth wouldn't agree to accompany him. He wouldn't have gone at all if she hadn't insisted. But now, the excitement of the opportunity made him believe she was right.

He wasn't even sure how this meeting would work since he'd let his agent go after he left UT. Tanner had given up on the entire political mess, but he was sure the man who worked for dozens of other coaches would hop right in with the knowledge he'd been offered an offensive coordinator job at such a young age. What agent wouldn't want that on their record?

A zap of excitement shot through him and he turned onto Volunteer Street. Not winning-play adrenaline, but definitely enough to make the hair stand at attention on his arms. Nyland Stadium stood like a beacon in the center of the university, pumping life into the campus. Football wasn't just a sport; it was the energy of Knoxville.

He parked his car, remembering the first day he'd arrived to coach. Driving onto the beautiful campus, he'd felt like he'd come home after a long sabbatical in the north. The warm southern sun on his face, friendly people who waved at every corner, the at-home feel of the Smoky Mountains in the back-drop. In that moment, he'd regretted remaining at Notre Dame for college, but they had been good to him, even after his injury. The grounds had been more foreign beauty, with an old-world feel, where UT welcomed you with its southern charm. He was a good ole southern boy grounded in his firm roots of farm life, but all those years ago, he'd thought he couldn't return home a loser when he'd left to be a winner.

With the afternoon sun piercing between the large brick buildings and the crowds of people swarming between classes, he thought he'd feel energized and excited, but he missed the quiet rippling of the lake and the sound of hummingbirds buzzing around his front porch eating sugar water from his mom's feeders.

This wasn't about farm life; this was about his career. His chance to prove himself worthy for the first time since his freshman year. Mary-Beth had opened a business and owned her life. He'd been assistant to someone else for years. Now, though, he could do something. He could mold an offensive line the way he wanted to while working with the Offensive Coordinator.

Jackson greeted him at the door with an outstretched hand. "Glad you could make it. This is a little unorthodox, but since this is a unique situation, I thought I'd have you come in to say hi to the coaches and chat with them for a bit."

"Sounds good to me." He followed the man to his future, leaving Mary-Beth, the farm, and Sugar Maple reluctantly behind.

"Don't tell them I said this, but this is a formality. The uppity-ups already decided this job is yours, and the coaches think you'd be able to slide into the former offensive coordinator's position since he left abruptly due to family obligations."

"I hope he's okay." Tanner remembered the man fondly. They'd worked together last year.

"Yes, all is good. His wife was transferred overseas, and he's decided it was the right move for the family. He'd been considering retiring for a while."

"Great."

"You ready?"

"Yes." He was more than ready. It was what he had set out to do years ago, and today, he'd be one of the youngest offensive coordinators in college football history. That would allow him to keep his head high for a long time.

* * *

THE GARDEN LOOKED like a set for the ending scene of a romance movie. The garland was strung through the wood of the arch trellis and the newly constructed pergola. Ms. Horton's wedding would be memorable. They'd waited decades to be together. They deserved this, so Mary-Beth put on a happy face and dove into work. It was nice to be out at the farm in the fresh air instead of the coffee shop for a change. There was no reason to be open anyway, with most of the town working on the farm.

"You don't have to be here. We'll cover for you," Carissa offered, holding a basket for Felicia.

"I wouldn't be anywhere else. Felicia, you've outdone yourself. How did you do all this?"

She eyed the tall, handsome, ex-con-turned-boyfriend who hammered away at the altar. A twinge of jealousy mixed with happiness for one of her best friends collided into a menagerie of emotions that took her breath.

Carissa placed the basket on the ground and touched Mary-Beth's shoulder. "You sure? We can totally cover for you."

"No, seriously. I want to be here." Mary-Beth went to work painting the barn with Stella and Jackie. Well, Jackie took on a more supervisory role.

Andy climbed the ladder to reach the beams, causing Mary-Beth's nerves to hitch. "You be careful up there. You're not invincible, you know."

"I hear you, Par-sis."

"Par-sis?" she asked.

Andy shrugged, paint falling from his brush into a squealing Jackie's hair. "Yeah, you're not just a sister. You're the closest thing I have to a parent but better. So, you're my parent sis, Par-sis."

"Clever, really," Jackie drawled while using a rag to try to rid her auburn hair of brown stain. "I thought you had house-broken him."

"You know, he's standing ten feet above you. I'd be careful what you say," Mary-Beth teased.

Jackie huffed and marched outside.

"Now that she's gone, spill it. How did Tanner's meeting go?"

Mary-Beth shrugged. "Don't know. He hasn't returned or called. I'm sure it went well and that's why he's still there."

"Really? Are you trying to convince us or yourself?" Stella gave her the hip out, I-know-you-too-well look.

Knox entered the barn with an apprehensive expression.

Mary-Beth dropped her paintbrush into the tray and wiped her hands on a rag, ready to escape the confines of chatter in the barn. "I'm sorry about the show."

Knox looked to Stella and then said in a rehearsed tone, "Don't worry about it. No big deal. I'll come up with a new angle."

The smell of paint fumes and disappointment made Mary-

Beth's stomach churn, so she escaped to the fresh air. Every-where she turned, there were more people giving her the sad, poor-girl-was-dumped look.

A car door slammed and her beath caught, but at the sight of Seth walking toward her, disappointment saturated her mood.

"Hey there. Can we talk?"

She shrugged. "Sure. What's up?"

He escorted her away from the crowd and the Sugar Maple gossip tree. "Listen, I'm sorry about what happened with Tanner. The guy's an idiot."

"Is that what you drove all the way out here to tell me in dress pants and an expensive shirt and tie?" she asked.

"No. I came out here to talk business with you."

"You did?" Before she knew it, she found herself leading him down the path to the tree house.

"Listen, I've been on the road and on planes for two solid days visiting various coffee shops. But there are none like your place. I'd like to start a chain of Maple Grounds but call it the Coffee Whisperer. You'll consult on all beverages and agree to tour once a year to create new blends during PR events."

"What? My little coffee shop is a small-town novelty. It can't be some sort of big chain."

"I know numbers, and I can tell you now that it can and it will give you enough money to hire help and retire early. Like twenty years early. I'll run all day-to-day business stuff, and you create the beverages and do the tour. That's it."

Her brain twisted around the idea and what it meant. As much as she loved her coffee shop, it was time to have some freedom. Working from four in the morning until nine in the evening, seven days a week, was starting to wear on her. Not to mention she wanted time to go visit Andy at whatever college he went to. "How long until I start seeing profits?"

"A year or so."

"And how large will the profits be?"

"Small in the beginning, but based on my analysis, it'll grow quickly. The coffee market is tough, but you have a unique spin, and people are tired of the same chain on every corner. It's a good time to invest in this, and it'll allow me to focus on what I want to do with the rest of my life. It's a win-win for us both."

She thought about the jealousy Tanner would feel with this arrangement, but he wasn't here to express his displeasure. And at the end of the year, when Andy went to college, she'd be able to visit Knoxville more often. "And you won't have any rights to my existing shop?"

"No, that will remain in your complete control. It'll all be in the contracts that you'll have your own lawyer look over."

She shot her hand out. "Deal."

"Great! I'll have the paperwork drawn up."

"Sounds good. That is, once I have a lawyer." She laughed. A floating kind of lightness—like she'd inhaled a hundred helium balloons—took over her body. In that moment, she didn't have to give up her financial independence, or any independence at all. She could have her man and never struggle the way her mother had. "Will you excuse me? There's something I have to do."

Without waiting for an answer, Mary-Beth darted to the not-so-secret hideout and climbed the steps to the tree house, fell to her knees, slid the secret door to the right, retrieved the tin box, and opened it. Inside sat the tarnished gold ring with diamond chips. The most beautiful sight she'd ever seen.

With shaking hands, she lifted it from the box and slid it

onto her ring finger. It didn't fit, though. It slid halfway on but wouldn't go over her knuckle.

"What are you doing?" Tanner's voice echoed in the small space, pounding against her psyche until it registered that he was in their tree house, not in Knoxville.

She tossed the tin box aside with a bang and crawled to his side, where he slipped in and sat on the floor. "Tanner. You don't have to choose between your dream and me. I don't have to choose either. We can have it all."

His gaze traveled from her head to her toes, as if he searched for the answers. He was breathing heavy from climbing the ladder, but she couldn't give him space to breathe, not when she needed to be near him, next to him. With him.

"What are you talking about?" he asked.

"I have an investor who is opening a coffee chain, and I can afford to hire help. We'll only have to do long distance for the rest of this year, and then I can come stay with you and come here to check on things once or twice a week."

"But you said you didn't want to be my football shadow, that you wanted to have your own accomplishments in life."

"I know what I said, but forget it. Tanner, I've made my choice. Andy is leaving, and I'll have the means to not give up my shop. But Tanner, despite my mom's warning, despite my fear of you leaving me behind, I know one thing. I don't want to live without you."

"You won't have to. I turned the job down." He shifted from his hip onto his knees, obviously trying to fit into the tiny space better.

"What are you talking about? It's your dream to be a head coach in college ball. You'd be so close."

"I have a new dream." His eyes dropped to her lips, and her body heated to campfire hot. "I've already spoken to the high school. You're looking at the new PE teacher and high school football coach."

"But—"

He cupped her cheek, brushing his thumb over her lips and distracting her. "I realized that even as offensive coordinator, I'll never feel the way I did coaching that high school game. Working as a team, inventing plays that fit these kids, working and helping mold them into men offers more adrenaline than any game I've ever played in."

She closed her eyes and leaned into his hand, willing his words to be true.

"But that isn't my dream."

She opened to find him moving from her, and she thought she'd die from the loss of contact. He pointed to her finger and then pulled a box from his pocket. "I think this will fit a little better and will be more appropriate for our age." A shining silver ring with a center diamond surrounded by pearls glistened in the dim light. "It was my grandmother's. My mother told me she saved it all these years for you."

"It's beautiful." Tears streamed down her face, but she didn't care. Before she put that ring on her finger, she needed to know for sure this was real. "Tanner…"

"Don't you see, Mary-Beth? You were and always will be my dream. Football means nothing when you're not in my life."

She lunged into him, knocking him back, and they tumbled to the floor. She kissed Tanner in a way that let him know he was the one and only man she had or ever would want in her life. She enjoyed the sweet caresses of his palm on her cheek, the feeling of his strong lips, probing, searching, claiming her. But most of all, when their passion settled and the sun faded in the sky, she fell into his arms and felt him pull her tight against him.

He whispered, "If you hold me, I'll never leave again."

EPILOGUE

THE WEDDING MARCH SOUNDED, and everyone stood from the rows of white picnic chairs separated by a single aisle. Mr. Strickland stood at the front, waiting for his bride forty plus years in the making. Mary-Beth was thankful she wouldn't have to wait that long. Tanner had wanted to marry her yesterday, but she'd convinced him to wait until the hoopla of Ms. Horton and Mr. Strickland's was over. Perhaps a spring wedding would be perfect. Besides, she'd want her mother and father there, and they couldn't get away until late spring or early summer.

Ms. Horton shuffled up the white paper rose petals–covered aisle. Her pale pink dress Jackie had constructed was tea length and had chiffon sleeves with white pearl buttons down the back. It fit Ms. Horton to perfection, and with the tiara Mary-Beth convinced her to wear, she looked like a queen.

Knox and Stella, Carissa and Drew, Felicia and Declan all sat in their row to the left and Jackie to their right. Alone. She was the last of the Fabulous Five to remain single. But the way

Firefighter Elijah Warner kept glancing across the aisle told Mary-Beth it might not be for long. They'd first met at Felicia's when her home was set on fire, and they'd been seen together at the football games. However, the thought of Jackie being with a man with kids sounded ludicrous. Of course, who would've thought that a football star who vowed to see the world would return to Sugar Maple and be happy? Life was funny that way.

When Ms. Horton and Mr. Strickland joined hands, the preacher began to speak about love surviving many obstacles in life and how their union was a great example of how God has a perfect plan and the right person for us. Of course, no one mentioned this was Mr. Strickland's fourth or fifth marriage, which didn't matter since before the first, he'd always been meant to be with Ms. Horton. Everyone knew that. Unfortunately, wrong decisions and life had gotten in their way for many years.

Mr. Strickland turned to the ring bearer and spoke in an unpolished tone, which was unlike him. It was precious to hear his voice crack with emotion and see his hands shake so much Ms. Horton had to help guide the ring on. How could the man be so nervous after dating for decades and being the player he'd once been?

Love did funny things to people.

Tanner held tight to Mary-Beth until the end of the ceremony, which concluded with thunderous applause that Creekside had to have heard. "It won't be long now until our wedding. You know, with me staying here, you don't have to work with Seth now."

"Why, Tanner McCadden, are you jealous?" Mary-Beth teased in her deepest southern drawl.

"Maybe."

The guests followed the happy couple out to the picnic area, where a potluck was already set out.

Tanner led her behind the shed and pressed her against the wall. "Just in case he tries to steal you away, remember this." He kissed her in a way that spoke of how he was here to stay and would never leave her side again. And she believed him.

"Hey, you two going to do that all day?" Andy rounded the corner, groaning. "They need the Coffee Whisperer for the final scenes of your segment."

Mary-Beth sighed, resting her head back against the siding with a clang. "Here we come."

"You sure we have to finish this show?" Tanner asked.

She took him by the hand. "I don't mind, now that it has a happy ending. Even if I never could figure out your drink."

They made their way behind the table, and the camera began to roll while she mixed up her own special coffee for a little energy boost before they began filming. After a few enjoyable sips, she set it aside and nodded that she was ready to roll. As she concocted the signature beverage for the wedding, one by one guests came to her table and took a cup with a nod and smile to the camera.

As rehearsed, she looked at the camera and hated that she'd be lying to people, but that was show biz. "And now it's time for the special drink I created for Tanner."

Knox waved like a ring master to everyone around. "I'll add in some commentary here. Tanner, take a drink and then look at the camera and say how much you love it."

He gave a curt nod and snagged a cup. Before she could tell him that it was her beverage, not the signature drink, he'd already pressed it to his lips. When he lowered the cup, she saw it. The joy in his face. She studied the cup and then him.

"Wow, this is perfect!" he exclaimed.

For a moment, she forgot they were rolling-and when she remembered, she didn't care. "But that wasn't your drink. That was mine."

He set it down and pulled her to him. "That's why it's perfect. It tastes like you." He claimed her lips, and she forgot all about production and filming and Knox and everything else around them, because she knew the truth. She and Tanner were perfect for each other.

"Cut. Perfect. That's a wrap. Dang, he's a good actor." Knox's words filtered in as Tanner pulled away and hugged her.

"That wasn't acting. She did it. She coffee whispered him." Stella's words made Mary-Beth giggle, but it was true. All that time she'd tried to find the perfect blend, but all she needed to do was be herself. That's what he'd always wanted... Her.

THE END

RECIPE

Recipe A recipe from the McCadden Farmhouse kitchen straight to your table. Homemade cornbread is a staple food on the McCadden farm, and this is Tanner's favorite evening snack.

- 1 cup cornmeal
- 1 cup all-purpose flour
- 1 teaspoon baking powder
- 1/2 teaspoon baking soda
- 1/8 teaspoon salt
- 1/2 cup unsalted butter, melted and slightly cooled
- 1/3 cup packed light brown sugar
- 1/3 cup white sugar
- 1 large egg
- 1 cup buttermilk, at room temperature

1. Preheat oven to 375 degrees F and grease 8-9 inch pan.

2. Whisk the cornmeal, flour, baking powder, baking soda, and salt together in a large bowl. Set aside.

3. Melt butter in large skillet. Remove from heat and stir in brown and white sugars and then let cool.

4. Add egg and beat until well blended.

5. Mix in buttermilk.

6. Pour the wet ingredients into the dry ingredients and whisk until combined. Avoid over-mixing.

7. Pour batter into prepared baking pan.

8. Bake for 20 minutes or until golden brown on top and the center is cooked through.

ABOUT THE AUTHOR

Ciara Knight is a USA TODAY Bestselling Author, who writes clean and wholesome romance novels set in either modern day small towns or wild historic old west. Born with a huge imagination that usually got her into trouble, Ciara is happy she's found a way to use her powers for good. She loves spending time with her characters and hopes you do, too.

ALSO BY

For a complete list of my books, please visit my website at www. ciaraknight.com. A great way to keep up to date on all releases, sales and prizes subscribe to my Newsletter. I'm extremely sociable, so feel free to chat with me on Facebook, Twitter, or Goodreads.

For your convenience please see my complete title list below, in reading order:

CONTEMPORARY ROMANCE

Winter in Sweetwater County

Spring in Sweetwater County

Summer in Sweetwater County

Fall in Sweetwater County

Christmas in Sweetwater County

Valentines in Sweet-water County

Fourth of July in Sweetwater County

Thanksgiving in Sweetwater County

Grace in Sweetwater County

Faith in Sweetwater County

Love in Sweetwater County

Sugar Maple Series

If You Love Me

If You Adore Me

If You Cherish Me

If You Hold Me

If You Kiss Me

Riverbend

In All My Wishes

In All My Years

In All My Dreams

In All My Life

A Christmas Spark

A Miracle Mountain Christmas

HISTORICAL WESTERNS:

McKinnie Mail Order Brides Series

Love on the Prairie

(USA Today Bestselling Novel)

Love in the Rockies

Love on the Plains

Love on the Ranch

His Holiday Promise

(A Love on the Ranch Novella)

Love on the Sound

Love on the Border

Love at the Coast

A Prospectors Novel

Fools Rush

Bride of America

Adelaide: Bride of Maryland

YOUNG ADULT:

Battle for Souls Series

Rise From Darkness

Fall From Grace

Ascension of Evil

The Neumarian Chronicles

Weighted

Escapement

Pendulum

Balance

Made in the USA
Columbia, SC
12 October 2022

69222104R00124